D

Comments on To

"Tom O'Connell connects with readers soul to
   soul...inspires."
--Jordan Rich, *WBZ News Radio 1030,* Boston

"It's the finest example of anyone writing on this
   subject."
--Don LaTulippe, *WPLM Radio*, Plymouth

"Your talk was warm and funny...You are a natural
   storyteller."
--Shirley Eastman, *Friends of the Cotuit Library*

"A page turner...mind boggling...a stunning view."
--Melora North, *Cape Cod Magazine*

"O'Connell writes compellingly."
--Melanie Lauwers, *Cape Cod Times*

"Thank you for your delightful presentation."
--Justine Bowen, *Irish American Club of Cape Cod*

"Very vivid...A fascinating read."
--Bob Silverberg, *Books & The World TV*

"Thank you for your delightful presentation...warmly
   received."
--Kathie Glynn, *Falmouth Public Library*

"Earthy dialogue sprinkled with wit, candor and
   affection."
--*The Dedham Times*

Quotes from the pages of Deviant Shelter:
Year Three of The New Social System
A Novel by Tom O'Connell

(Chapter 1) Video units suspended from the ceiling in the three corners of the triangle provide constant surveillance of his activities. Each unit includes a video receiver and player, camera, microphone and amplifier.

There are no reflective surfaces in the triangle. The television receiver high above him does not reflect any images of the room. His word processor screen is permanently covered with a substance that protects the machine from harm and also eliminates reflections. The bright overhead lighting is diffused so that even a puddle on the floor will not give back a reflection. There is no way for him to observe his own appearance.

(Chapter 2) "Life at the orphanage was totally disciplined. The Brothers had a complete book publishing operation and every orphan was part of the enterprise. When I was only five years old I was working in the book bindery carrying glue pots to the cover machine. By the time I was seven I was running a cover machine. At nine I was an apprentice to a typesetter. I didn't know what being a child was. I only knew about work.

"Up at dawn every day. Scrubbing floors and cleaning up before breakfast. Oatmeal for breakfast. Daily Mass in the chapel. School. A light lunch. Working in the bindery. Religious instruction. Memorizing prayers. Singing hymns. A skimpy piece of meat and bland vegetables for supper. Evening Benediction. Assigned reading. Baths. Sleep. Day after day. On and on. The same pattern."

(Chapter 3) "Ah, you're way over the border, Fayne. One time I come in and you're wild and raunchy and another time you're some kind of religious fanatic. I don't know why I even bother talking to you."

The Doctor remained silent as they walked along the corridor. Then there was a slight tremor and the sound of distant rumbling. "Probably some of those FRN sympathizers planting their bombs. Or maybe another one of those demonstrations with fireworks about that writer Lance Crowne. They want that traitor dead, Fayne. I don't think they'd be satisfied if he went to a patho shelter for retraining or reorganizing his brain. No. They want him dead."

(Chapter 4) The deviant's voice began to fade as he recited quietly. Then he raised his voice so I could hear him continue: "And admirably schooled in every grace: In fine, we thought that he was everything…So on we worked, and waited for the light, And went without the meat, and cursed the bread; And Richard Cory, one calm summer's night, Went home and put a bullet through his head."

(Chapter 5) "Now, Doctor, let us proceed with The Unveiling. During our last session you were telling me that you were practicing celibacy to avoid Anna's domineering approach to sexual intimacy."

"Yes, that was the way it was for a while. And then a kind of seduction began. As I was growing more humble and less professorial and more Christian in a down-to-earth way, Anna was growing less like a radical feminist and very methodically making herself more alluring. She was changing her appearance to tempt me and invited me to her room late at night. She would greet me with nothing on except her sheer lingerie. But I hadn't forgotten the pain of her previous scorn and abuse, so I maintained my celibacy."

(Chapter 6) He cupped his right hand around his right ear. "You say you're the abandoned bride? What bride? I can hear you, but I can't see you. Why can't I see you?" He looked toward the velvet wall. "There. I see you now, with your white dress.

"You say I betrayed you? I never betrayed anybody. You saw God on a crucifix? Never! Anna who? I don't know any Anna." He began rubbing his eyes hard and shaking his head rapidly. Then he started pushing his hands away from his face, as if pushing an object or a person, and he shouted, "Get out of my eyes!"

(Chapter 7) "Doctor Fayne," interjected The Keeper over the amplification system. "This is not a chapel. We are a nonsectarian institution. Have I not told you that there are no more religious institutions in the Provinces? You are here to complete The Unveiling, and you would be well advised to proceed immediately, without further impulsive actions, to the set of three steps so that we may continue where we left off during our previous session."

(Chapter 8) He stood there a while, and when no other frightening visions erupted in front of him, he carefully slid down and seated himself in the scoop-back chair, looked at the velvet wall, sighed, and said angrily, "Damn snakes, wolves, triangles, circles and squares. Never any peace." He got up fast, went to the bookcase, pushed aside the soiled copies of Goethe's *Faust* and *The Basic Writings of Sigmund Freud*, then grabbed the clean white-covered book with the red and black lettering: *The Prince*, by Machiavelli.

(Chapter 9) When Doctor Fayne gave visual proof that he would now be compliant enough to continue, The Keeper said, "During your last session with me, you were telling me about the four variations of Anna...the conservative social worker, the pleasure addict, the woman in the white dress who thought she was your abandoned bride, and the depressed widow. You were saying that Anna the widow was in such a state of torment that her facial structure was changing. What kind of a look did she have, Doctor?"

Deviant Shelter:
Year Three of
The New Social System
(NSS)

A Novel
By Tom O'Connell

Sanctuary Unlimited
(www.sanctuary777.com)

Deviant Shelter:
Year Three of The New Social System (NSS)
A Novel by Tom O'Connell

Published in the United States by
Sanctuary Unlimited
P.O. Box 25, Dennisport, MA 02639
info@sanctuary777.com

This book was printed in the United States of America.

To order additional copies of this book, contact your bookseller and refer to Ingram Book Company or go to amazon.com or Sanctuary Unlimited's sanctuary777.com.

Copyright 2010 Tom O'Connell
ISBN: 978-0-9827766-0-5

Dedicated

To lovers of personal freedom and autonomy who have difficulty with arbitrary authority and find it painful to adapt to systems that attempt to dehumanize participants.

~~~~~~~

"In the centre of the castle of Brahman, our own body, there is a small shrine in the form of a lotus flower, and within can be found a small space. We should find who dwells there, and we should want to know him."
--Chandogya Upanishad 8:1

~~~~~~~

Thanks

To the God of Love and Truth and to all those who have helped me to find my way through various life passages, challenging transitions, endurance tests, and intriguing mazes during this adventurous journey that we call life.

Deviant Shelter:
Year Three of The New Social System (NSS)
A Novel
By Tom O'Connell

Synopsis

Length: 60,000 words
Time: Future
Avernus Province, The New Social System (NSS)

A Kafka epigraph hints at the tone of this suspense novel about an alienated man in a totalitarian society that may now be forming. Here is the Kafka quote: "If the book we are reading does not wake us, as with a fist hammering on our skull, why then do we read it? A book must be an ice-axe to break the sea frozen inside us."

The story is seen through the eyes of a psychotherapist who dispassionately observes the central character through video units. Each chapter is a case summary reporting the "deviant's" behavior.

Here are the opening lines that set the scene: "This is my first assignment at the new Deviant Shelter in Bentham. It is a pleasure to work in a psychological deviant shelter with the latest technology.

"It is Year Three of The New Social System (NSS) and all mental health institutions, prisons and correctional facilities in the United Econocratic Provinces have been replaced with deviant shelters for those who do not fit the government's current definition of 'normal.'

"It is a pleasure to work in a psychological deviant shelter with the latest technology. Doctor Wylie Fayne, who is the first resident to experience our new Time Void Therapy, is in the Total Scrutiny Wing of the shelter that has been designed as a pyramid.

"The Doctor has been fitted with new neuropsychological implants (NPI) and his therapy is designed to return him to a healthy mental condition. He has completed his first session.

"The resident deviant is in complete solitude. Time has been eliminated from his environment. He exists in extreme isolation with his jumbled thoughts, impressions, voices and scenes."

When we first observe the "deviant" whose mental condition is in question, he is in his triangular-shaped space going through one of his disorderly phases. We see and hear him act out angrily in an apparently insane way.

We watch his bizarre actions and we see how he reacts to his only human contact. We observe his reaction to his attendant Sumner's report that the whole country is outraged by the writing of an author named Lance Crowne and that "the people" want to see him dead because he has written a treasonous book titled *The Betrayal*. Among other goals, Doctor Fayne's therapy is designed to verify whether or not the deviant is the author of the subversive literature.

Following the deviant into an automated cleaning room where he is bathed in the same way a car is washed, we are with him as he is led down corridors to a distant room where an entity called The Keeper is going to have a "therapeutic dialogue" with him.

We feel his helplessness and his anger as he tries to resist the treatment program that has been designed to bring him to a condition described as "normal."

In The Keeper's chamber, he is motivated to kneel and face a golden screen. The Keeper's voice comes at him from that screen and, with the assistance of medications, he is prompted to tell his true life story.

At a certain point, the drugs wear off and he returns to his earlier behavior. Then he is taken back to his solitary triangle by Sumner to await a future visit with The Keeper.

The next time we observe Doctor Fayne he has shifted to an opposite phase. He is now neat, clean, orderly and religiously pious. Acting as if he is hosting an inspirational television program, we see him talk directly to the camera. The deviant's orderly and disorderly phases wrap around the core story, which is a personal narration by the deviant about his own life. The development of this story is guided by the unseen Keeper's questions.

We are introduced in this tale to the possibilities of dehumanization that exist in conformist, authoritarian societies where an individual who is uncomfortable with the system can rapidly be transformed into a non-person.

As the core story unfolds, the central character reflects on his past. We see how Doctor Fayne, prior to his confinement, apparently became progressively alienated from the world in which he lived as a college philosophy professor frustrated with the trends of modern times.

Learning that he has published his own provocative newsletter as a vehicle to comment critically on the problems of the times, we may wonder if perhaps he is, after all, the seditious writer who must die.

In the orderly and disorderly phases in his triangle we see Doctor Fayne portray an angry rebel and a serene monk. As we read, we become part of a mental dance of clashing ideas. And we also see a love story develop within the core story. Clues about the love story are sprinkled into the scenes. Also, we are exposed to the possibilities of alcoholism in Doctor Fayne and mental disease in his wife Anna.

Deviant Shelter poses questions on the meaning of life both for an individual and for a member of society. It poses questions on the pursuit of goals and how much of a person's soul must be sacrificed to win the prizes. And it poses questions about the value of life in a society in which a person who questions a collectivist system may be viewed as a "deviant" and stripped of all dignity in an attempt to shape him into a conforming member of the group.

The novel contains elements of a tragic love affair, split personalities, psychotherapy, spiritual factors, and questions about the future of this planet. These elements are woven into a fabric that ranges from the bizarre to the sublime.

"If the book we are reading does not wake us, as with a fist hammering on our skull, why then do we read it? So that it shall make us happy? Good God, we would also be happy if we had no books, and such books as make us happy we could, if need be, write ourselves.

"But what we must have are those books which come upon us like ill-fortune, and distress us deeply, like the death of one we love better than ourselves, like suicide.

"A book must be an ice-axe to break the sea frozen inside us." --Franz Kafka, letter at age 20

Epigraphs

- "To different minds, the same world is a hell, and a heaven." --Ralph Waldo Emerson
- "Anyone who really knows the human psyche will agree with me when I say that it is one of the darkest and most mysterious regions of our experience." --C.G. Jung
- "Instead of disappearing, authority has made itself invisible. Instead of overt authority, 'anonymous' authority reigns. It is disguised as common sense, science, psychic health, normality, public opinion...There is nobody and nothing to fight back against." --Erich Fromm
- "It is at once our loneliness and our dignity to have an incommunicable personality that is ours, ours alone and no one else's, and will be so forever." --Thomas Merton
- "The face of truth remains hidden behind a circle of gold. Unveil it, O God of light, that I who love the true may see!" --Isa Upanishad
- "Good is set against evil, and life against death, so also is the sinner against a just man. And so look upon all the works of the Most High, two and two, and one against another." --Ecclesiasticus, 33:15

"Anyone who really knows the human psyche will agree with me when I say that it is one of the darkest and most mysterious regions of our experience."
—C. G. Jung

Deviant Shelter:
Year Three of
The New Social System
(NSS)
A Novel by Tom O'Connell

1

Case Report
Deviant: Fayne, Wylie, Ph.D.
Number: I
Shelter: Bentham Deviant Shelter
Province: Avernus
Housing: Total Scrutiny
Therapy: Time Void
Technique: Observation and dialogue
Condition: To be ascertained.

Summary of Introductory Session Number 1

This is my first assignment at the new Deviant Shelter in
Bentham. It is a pleasure to work in a psychological deviant
shelter with the latest technology.

It is Year Three of The New Social System (NSS) and all
mental health institutions, prisons and correctional facilities
in the United Econocratic Provinces have been replaced with

deviant shelters for those who do not fit the government's current definition of 'normal.'

It is an honor to serve in a psychological deviant shelter with the latest technology. Doctor Wylie Fayne, who is the first resident to experience our new Time Void Therapy, is in the Total Scrutiny Wing of the shelter that has been designed as a pyramid.

The Doctor has been fitted with new neuropsychological implants (NPI) and his therapy is designed to return him to a healthy mental condition. He has completed his first session.

The resident deviant is in complete solitude. Time has been eliminated from his environment. He exists in extreme isolation with his jumbled thoughts, impressions, voices and scenes.

The professor has the distinction of being the first to experience the new Time Void Therapy and appropriate neuropsychological implants (NPI) have been attached to his nervous system. The goal of his therapy is to move him toward an acceptable mental condition so he can be useful to the government.

The clinical record indicates that the deviant became traumatized and delusional after he was attacked by an angry mob. The crowd believed he was the unknown author of a treasonous book that was savagely critical of The New Social System. After his rescue from the violent mob, he was admitted to this new psychological deviant shelter for observation and therapy.

The deviant seems to have no consistent world view because he appears to have no clear chain of memories that work sequentially from a beginning to an end. It is as if someone has erased his memory and replaced it with a scattering of impressions, scenes, and feelings that have no logical connection with one another. These images appear to be like dream or nightmare images. Also, he sometimes responds to voices that praise, curse, or condemn him.

He has compulsive urges, too. One of them is his repetition of words and actions ad infinitum. For example, he fills pages of paper with one-line messages during long hours at the word processor.

Based on my review of initial video screening of his behavior during his first days here, I believe his current mental existence is a chaos of opposite factors. His language is either extremely negative or exceptionally positive. His personal hygiene is either unkempt or fanatically neat. And he is now in one of his negative, unkempt phases.

When I began my first formal observation today, his triangular quarters were littered with balls of printed paper that he had crumpled and heaved at random over his shoulder. There were puddles on the floor from splashed water and from bodily functions. There was also garbage here and there, from meals that had not suited his taste.

He seemed to be oblivious to his surroundings as he sat in his scoop-back chair, with eyes closed and head hanging down so that the tip of his black-and-gray beard was touching the top of his bony chest.

Suddenly his eyes opened and his clenched fist waved at a video camera in one of the corners of his triangle and he shouted, "Get lost!" His dark brown eyes were flashing with intensity as he repeated the shout and leaped from his chair so fast that his knee-length gray smock went flying up around his hips. Then, with his cloth-slippered feet, he kicked his way in a straight line toward the electrified steel door which is activated by sensors.

Doctor Fayne worked up some phlegm, coughed it onto his tongue, and let the wad of spit fly onto the door. On contact, the sensors were activated and the spit sizzled into a combination of smoke and steam. He watched the spit disappear and shook his head. Then he pounded on the door with his fists and was repelled backward forcefully by the electric shock. He muttered, "I'm stuck." Then he repeated this sequence of behavior several times.

Finally, he went to the word processor and examined the printed manuscript page. It was nearly filled with the line, "God help me!" He continued to type the same phrase until the sheet was filled. Then he stared at the paper for a while, yanked it out of the printer, crumpled it, and threw it over his shoulder, muttering, "There's something screwed up here."

Hitching up his smock, he rubbed his genitals with part of the material, took another piece of paper, and began typing on the word processor keyboard again. He went through the same cycle of behavior, filling the paper with the same phrase, throwing it away, and making the same comment. Eventually, he returned to his scoop-back chair and slumped into it with a massive sigh.

He fixed his eyes on the black velvet wall opposite him and sat quietly for a moment. The deep vertical crease in his forehead, extending up from the bridge of his nose, flattened out as his breathing slowed. Then he tensed up again as he looked at the camera through which I was observing him.

"Why are you doing this to me?" he shouted. "What have I done to deserve this?" He shook his head. "No answer. Never any answer."

Then he clutched his head, squinted, and moaned as his face contorted with pain. Trying to get up, he did not make it. He vomited onto the floor and some of the mess covered his own feet. Apparently, it was another migraine headache.

Again he slumped back into the chair and began to relax. Then he sat up straight and muttered, "Ouch! Damn! It's you again, Flea!"

Pulling the flea from his forearm, he held it between his index finger and thumb and said, "Why do you keep attaching yourself to me? I don't need you. What if I were to squeeze you till there was no you left? Would you like that? Hah. You have courage, don't you? Or are you just ignorant?

"Where are the others? Sleeping? The three of you can be

irritating, you know. I want to be alone now, so will you tell the others I'm in no mood for company today? I have some very important work to do and have no time for social niceties.

"Did you hear what I said? I have no time! Do you get the subtle humor? No time? I am receiving Time Void Therapy, so I have no time. Do you think that's funny? No. Your sense of humor is not highly developed. You make a very unsatisfactory companion. Go! Leave me now! Let me be."

He flicked the flea in the direction of the bunk. Once again, he gazed at the black velvet wall where he apparently saw a form of some kind. Then he muttered, "Yes, I know. You're absolutely right. How could anyone question your sincerity? I do understand. Maybe you should try..."

Pausing, he whispered, "Listen to it hiss. Like a snake." He closed his eyes tightly, clamped his hands over his ears, pressed his lips together, and hunched up in a ball in his chair. Then the high pressure hose nozzles up above spurted a flow of chemically treated water throughout the entire triangle. It drenched him and spun him around in his chair several times. Then the water stopped, the chair stopped whirling, and a rush of hot air filled the room, rapidly drying everything in it, including Doctor Fayne.

The protective technology surrounding all equipment in the triangle worked very efficiently. The electrification of the steel door was not affected by the spraying action, nor was any harm done to the newly designed word processing equipment. The debris that had been littering the floor was compressed into a soggy but cleansed mass near the drain in the corner. The cleaning operation was flawless. It is a tribute to the engineers who designed this facility.

After the spraying had stopped, Doctor Fayne shouted, "Damn your spray!" He remained seated in his scoop-back gray plastic chair shouting at the nearest overhead video camera, "You're killing me! You're wiping me out!"

He paused and as he clenched his teeth I saw his jaw muscles ripple. He was experiencing great tension. Shaking his head in dismay, he shot a fearful glance at the camera. "Why are you wiping me out?" he asked with a shrug. "No answer. They never answer."

He closed his eyes, breathed a heavy sigh as he slumped back into the chair, slowed his breathing, and seemed to be going into a state of complete rest. Then he opened his eyes and grunted. "Damn them and their triangle." He sighed again, closed his eyes, and said no more. His breathing slowed as his hands rested limply in his lap. There was complete silence in the triangle now, other than his breathing.

I am impressed with the design of Doctor Fayne's three-walled, pie-shaped room with no windows. The concrete walls are about five meters long. Two walls are a dull gray texture. The remaining wall is covered with permanently inlaid black velvet that seems even blacker as it contrasts with the rest of the room that is predominantly gray. It is quite suitable for our purposes.

In front of the black velvet wall, mounted on a solid plastic pedestal a little to the right of the wall's center, there is a free-standing green-and-silver dart board for the Doctor's therapeutic recreational use. During the observation, I saw that the three green darts were resting in the bull's-eye. The darts are plastic and fitted with heads that stick to the board by a combination of magnetism and friction.

The Doctor's triangle is compact and utilitarian, with most objects fixed in place securely. The only mobile items I observed are such things as his clothing, towels and linen, the books in his bookcase, his word processor paper, his toilet tissue, and the three darts.

Even the plastic meal trays that carry his food to him on a dumbwaiter are fitted with lightweight but unbreakable plastic chains that can only be stretched as far as the top of his utility table.

Video units suspended from the ceiling in the three corners of the triangle provide constant surveillance of his activities. Each unit includes a video receiver and player, camera, microphone and amplifier.

There are no reflective surfaces in the triangle. The television receiver high above him does not reflect any images of the room. His word processor screen is permanently covered with a substance that protects the machine from harm and also eliminates reflections. The bright overhead lighting is diffused so that even a puddle on the floor will not give back a reflection. There is no way for him to observe his own appearance.

Every item he needs for his basic existence is included in the triangle. Push-button shower. Toilet. Refuse disposal system. Drainage. Lighting. Ventilation. Washbowl. Blow-drier. Water bubbler. Bunk bed. Chair. Stool. Bookcase. Electronic word processing computer and printer.

There is no way for the Doctor to escape the video cameras. There is no partition in the triangle. Nor is there any space under the bunk bed, which is permanently fixed to the floor. The only way in or out of the triangle is through an electrified solid steel door that has a one-way viewing device so that only those outside can look in. Doctor Fayne cannot see beyond his triangular space.

The television receiver, which may be utilized later in therapy, currently provides neither picture nor sound. Nor is there anything in his space to give any indication of time. There is no compromise in his therapy. Time is completely missing. And there are no outside sensations that have any regularity. Even the visits from his only human contact are made at random.

As my first observation continued, Doctor Fayne sat with eyes closed. His breathing was almost stopped when a clicking sound broke the deep silence. It was followed by the electronic buzz that comes before the door slides open.

The Doctor kept his eyes closed and waited. As the attendant's footsteps approached him, he continued to keep his eyes closed. Then the attendant stood in front of him and said, "Fayne, who are you trying to fool? I know you're awake." Doctor Fayne opened his eyes slowly, looked up, and said, "Oh. It's you..."

"Right, Fayne. It's me. Sumner."

The Doctor gave Sumner a contemptuous look, with clenched teeth. Then there was a long silence. As for the attendant, his appearance was excellent. His uniform was functional. The endless plastic belt around the waist seems ideally suited for the lock-switch electronic keys which adjust temperatures and lights and open doors. I noted that the belt also has small pockets attached to it for medication cartridges and is fitted with a secure holster for the medication gun.

The selection of the attendant was ideal. He is about as opposite to Doctor Fayne as a human being can be. He is dull and witless while the Doctor's intelligence at times borders on brilliance. The Doctor has dark brown eyes, a broad forehead, and a bony bearded face. Sumner has vacant blue eyes, stares in an unblinking manner, has a low forehead, and his face is clean-shaven.

Doctor Fayne's complexion is pale while Sumner's complexion is sallow. Doctor Fayne's frame is long and thin while Sumner is short, rugged, and broad-shouldered. The Doctor has gray streaks in his black hair. Sumner has uninterrupted blackness in his thick hair and sideburns. The Doctor's facial features are symmetrical. Sumner has a parrot nose and a drooping right eyelid that gives his left eye the impression that it is bulging. I cannot imagine an attendant more suited to our purposes.

Sumner confronted the Doctor about ignoring his presence. "I'm nobody's fool, Fayne. I knew you weren't sleeping."

The Doctor responded, "Nobody's fool? No, you're a jewel. Especially when you drool. Congratulations, Slumner, and may your tribe increase."

"Tribe? I have no tribe. And the name's Sumner, not Slumner. How many times do I have to tell you that, Fayne? Can't you remember anything? "

The Doctor remained silent as his attendant examined the triangle, sniffed a pile of debris, and complained about having no cleaning to do. "They flooded you again, huh Fayne?"

Doctor Fayne continued to remain silent as Sumner filled the disposal bin with the soggy litter and discharged the refuse through the trap leading to a chute connecting with the central disposal area. The equipment functioned perfectly.

Sumner told the Doctor how filthy it must have been in his triangle to need the cleaning operation. "The water guns don't flood the place till the stench gets more than most people can stand, you know. I guess there's no stench too much for your nose, huh Fayne?"

The attendant's face was completely without emotion as he made these statements to the Doctor. Combining limited intelligence, vulgarity, flat emotions, and humorlessness, Sumner appears to very satisfactorily fulfill the criteria we established for his position. Also, his lengthy experience at a pathological deviant shelter should be very beneficial.

"Fayne, if you played your cards right you'd be out of this place in no time. But I guess you don't know any better."

"I don't play cards, Slumner," replied the Doctor. "I've given them up, you see. Blackjack! I win! You lose!" He laughed derisively at Sumner.

Sumner replied, "You don't know what end is up, Fayne."

The Doctor kept repeating "Blackjack! I win! You lose!"

Then something attracted his attention as he looked toward the black velvet wall. "You say your name is Anna? I don't know any Anna. Failed you? How could I have failed you if I don't even know you? How could I...gone. No answer for my questions. Never any answer."

Sumner asked, "Are you seeing things, Fayne? Well, you better get moving. The Kuh... Kuh...Keeper wants to see you in his chamber and he doesn't wait for anybody, Fayne." Sumner's voice was tremulous as he spoke.

'I'he doctor replied, "Sweeper? Is that what you said, Slumner?"

"I said Kuh…Kuh…Keeper, Fayne. If you don't get moving you're going to regret it. You'll activate one of the implanted non-cooperation chips in your NPI."

"I'm rising and moving, Slumner. Slumner says to rise. Fayne rises. Simple transaction."

When Doctor Fayne stood up he was about a head higher than his attendant. This did not intimidate Sumner, who was pointing toward the electrified steel door. When activated by a quick wave, Sumner's hand could send electronic impulses to a variety of devices designed to provide security as well as electrical motivation to the deviant.

Sumner activated the door and motivated the Doctor to enter the dull silver-gray corridor, which is also without windows and very effectively covered by video units making uninterrupted surveillance possible.

"We're going to The Clean Room," Sumner explained.

The Doctor trembled visibly. "The Clean Room? Do you mean the death chamber? Is this the end of me? Am I meeting my Maker?"

"No, Fayne, you're meeting your Kuh...Kuh...Keeper. But you've got to get cleaned up first. You have to be spotless before you visit."

"What does this Keeper person look like?"

"Who knows? Nobody sees the Kuh... Kuh...Keeper and lives to talk about it, Fayne. If you see him, then I think your next stop's going to be The Trap. Then maybe I'll get to see you again...in the morgue. It's going to be part of my job here, taking care of the morgue. I think I'm going to like it there. I'm expecting to meet a nice class of people, if you know what I mean."

"Yes, I know what you mean, Slumner. You mean you're a sadistic creep."

Ignoring the insult, Sumner ordered, "Move a little faster, Fayne. We don't want to keep the Kuh...Kuh...Keeper waiting. I never saw anybody as slow as you. Are you slow on that word processor, too? What are you trying to write, Fayne? Your last will and testament?"

"No, it's your last will and testament, Slumner! Hah. Only kidding. Actually, I'm doing my Shakespeare routine. I'm writing about time. The time is out of joint here. And this joint is out of time."

"Too bad you've lost your marbles, Fayne. So, you think you're a writer, huh? What kind of writer are you, Fayne? The kind they're yelling about all around the Provinces?"

The Doctor made no response to Sumner's comments and Sumner persisted. "Ever hear of a writer named Lance Crowne? He's going to die. They're marching up and down the streets all over the Provinces saying he's got to die."

After a brief silence, the Doctor shouted, "Die? Piece of pie. One thing's sure. We can't deny. We have to die!"

"Crowne wrote this book everyone hates, Fayne. *The Betrayal.* They're doing demonstrations all over the Provinces about it. Never saw so many angry people since we changed to the peace and justice of The New Social System. If they find him, they'll kill him. I've never seen anything like it. They're really furious at this guy."

As they walked along the corridor, with the Doctor in front of his attendant, the deviant responded, "What's a little killing among friends, Slumner?"

"If the mobs get him, they'll tear his balls off. But if our health people get him to a shelter they'll help him get normal. Like they're going to help you get normal. Remember our motto in this psycho deviant shelter, 'We Are Concerned.' What kind of a doc are you, Fayne?"

"I'm a resident Doc, Slumner. I'm a resident deviant Doc. With no clock. Or am I a deviant resident? In any case, I'm a deviation from the norm, Slumner. I have no form without the norm."

"You going to start that rhyming thing again, Fayne? That's way over the border. It's pretty psycho and pretty neurotic."

"Neurotic? New rotic? Or neuralgia? New ralgia? Horatio Alger. A new Alger. A newer Alger. Neuralgia! Hah!"

"I guess you're a lost cause, Fayne."

"You should know, Slumner. With your smock and your key belt and vacuum, I must certainly applaud your rank in this tank no matter how odd. Why, you're halfway up the ladder to God!"

This kind of exchange continued as the two moved toward The Clean Room. There were no gaps in my observation during their walk. The cameras are located exceptionally well. On entering The Clean Room from the corridor, the video units cover the transition very effectively, as they do in the room. The efficient cleaning apparatus operates like a car wash, and its design seems to bring a minimum of discomfort during the washing process.

Doctor Fayne was a bit reluctant to undress himself. But Sumner prepared him by shooting the blue medication into his arm. "This will calm you down for the wash and for your little visit with the Kuh...Kuh...Keeper."

As the washing process began, the resident was strapped into an individual capsule-shaped container which was then set in motion. This reminder was given to him by Sumner: "Remember to hold your breath during the wash cycles."

During those cycles, the Doctor was sprayed with liquid soap in a way that was much more hygienically thorough than the washing he received while his triangle was being sprayed. During the rinse cycles he was sprayed with high velocity warm water. At the end of the line he was blasted with alternating currents of hot, warm and cool air.

When the machinery stopped, he was lying limp but spotlessly clean in the bottom of his capsule, with his eyes closed and his hands covering his ears.

"Come on, Fayne. You aren't dead, are you?"

The Doctor rose without a word, followed Sumner's instructions, put on his clean smock and slippers, and once again continued his journey along the corridor to The Keeper's chamber. He was completely silent now.

They soon reached the corridor that ran at an angle to the main corridor which, if one kept walking straight ahead, went off into the darkness. "Turn right here," said Sumner.

First the deviant paused, looked as if he might continue straight ahead along the main corridor, and then accepted Sumner's instruction.

"I've got to stop here, Fayne. Nobody goes down the Kuh...Kuh...Keeper's corridor without a special invitation, so play your cards right, and maybe I'll see you again. I think I'm getting used to you."

The Keeper's voice came over the amplifier from the video unit overhead. "You may go now, Sumner. Come right ahead to my chamber, Doctor Fayne. Come toward my golden door."

Doctor Fayne began moving cautiously toward the golden door. Then there was a click, a buzz, and a hum. And The Keeper's golden door slid open.

"Come in!" ordered The Keeper. "I have been waiting for you, Doctor."

Case Report Disposition: Observation to be continued.

2

Case Report
Deviant: Fayne, Wylie, Ph.D.
Number: 1
Shelter: Bentham Deviant Shelter
Province: Avernus
Housing: Total Scrutiny
Therapy: Time Void
Technique: Observation and Dialogue
Condition: To be ascertained.

Summary of Session Number 2

As I observed Doctor Fayne, he appeared fearful and was moving very slowly into The Keeper's chamber. When he shuffled through the entrance, he was startled by the automated medication guns that shot another dose of the blue tranquilizer solution into his right arm, followed by a shot of the pink memory stimulator solution into his left arm. The equipment functioned with maximum efficiency while causing minimum discomfort to the deviant.

As the door slid shut behind Doctor Fayne, he was confined in the most modern therapeutic dialogue chamber it has ever been my pleasure to experience. The triangular chamber is hygienically spotless. The lighting is bright. The complete absence of windows maintains our wish to remove all outside stimulation. The dull gold color of all surfaces in the chamber provides the effect our committee recommended to the architects.

The golden translucent wall that forms the base of the triangle is covered with a fine-meshed glittering golden screen providing the illusion that there may be still another chamber behind it. At the center of that wall is a large blurry golden circle that seems to have within it a variety of mysterious, indefinable shapes. It will suit our purposes well.

After stepping into the chamber, the deviant halted abruptly, examined his surroundings, stared at the video units suspended above, looked at the golden translucent wall, and then focused on the set of padded kneeling steps in the center of the room.

The steps are exactly as specified in our instructions. Golden plastic padding was used. The electronic elevator apparatus makes movement possible from one step to another with or without the deviant's consent. The large oval lustrous golden velvet rug surrounding the steps had the anticipated effect.

Doctor Fayne moved toward it with a look of fear and anticipation. Then he set his right foot on the edge of the rug and The Keeper's voice said firmly, "Stop!"

The Doctor squinted at the center of the golden screen where the voice seemed to be coming from. Then he made an obscene gesture with his right hand, lifted his foot from the rug, and slammed his foot down on the rug in defiance. Immediately, his foot was repelled at such high speed that his leg flew upward and his knee contacted his chin with enough impact to leave him stunned.

"God! I've cooked my own goose," he muttered as he took a step backward on the metallic floor.

The Keeper instructed him. "You are never to step on the velvet rug without my express permission. You must respect the authority of your Keeper, Doctor Fayne. If you insist on defying me you will bring yourself intense pain directly related to your transgressions.

"You have within your brain one of several state-of-the-art neuropsychological implants that we have provided for you. The NPI limits your behavior to a range that is not excessive. When you exceed that range the implant triggers painful reactions within your central nervous system. So, in a true sense, you cause your own pain by your own behavior. We who are trying to help you do not need to punish you in any way for acting foolishly. It is you who punish yourself. So the choice is yours."

Doctor Fayne shouted, "Get lost! Take your authority and shove it! You sound like a recording, damn it! What I can't see, I pay no attention to. So just get lost!"

As the last word was spoken, a resounding amplification of the Doctor's own words reverberated back at him and drilled into his ears at an unbearable decibel level. His face became contorted with pain. His eyes closed. His hands pressed against his ears. He began to gag. "Hrgh! Argh!" He let out a horrified screech. Then the sound subsided. The vertical crease in the center of his forehead began to smooth out. And the contortions of his pain-racked face lessened.

The Keeper explained, "We have no wish to punish you here, Doctor Fayne. We are dedicated to restoring you to health. At this time you are an enigma to us. Even the monitors we have surgically implanted throughout your body are not yet providing us with clues to your deviation from the acceptable norm. But rest assured that we will continue to help you become healthy. We are prepared to utilize Time Void Therapy indefinitely as we observe you and provide dialogue with you. But at some point, if you do not respond, we will have to ..."

"You can take your so-called dialogue and insert it in your own rectum if you have one!" shouted the deviant. No sooner had the words come out of his mouth than his voice amplified back at him with the same painful effect as the previous time.

In a very modulated voice, The Keeper said, "The tranquilizers will take effect soon, Doctor. You will be calmer then. Remember that we are here to help you. Our motto is 'We Are Concerned.' We wish to return you to normalcy. We care about you deeply. Trust us. The only pain you feel will be due to your own excesses, I assure you."

The Doctor replied, "If I don't cooperate, do you operate?

If I don't talk, do I take a long walk? To the Trap? Like a sap? Will I die? Like a fly? Oh my, oh my."

"Now, Doctor Fayne, you must not think in such negative terms. Please discount much of what Sumner says to you. He has a tendency to exaggerate. He speculates about things he knows nothing about. I am your friend, your therapist, your Keeper. My intention is to restore you to health. But if we fail, or if you become too difficult to handle, we may have to transfer you from this Psychological Deviant Shelter to a Pathological Deviant Shelter. It depends on your progress."

Doctor Fayne began to tremble. Then he muttered several inaudible sentences to himself.

"Our therapy is in your best interest," said The Keeper. "Trust us."

"Ah-hah-hah!" Doctor Fayne began laughing hysterically. "You're very funny." He laughed louder and louder. "Oh, boy, Ah-hah-hah! Help me? Best interest? Trust us? Ah-hah-hah!" His laughter was amplified many times over and soon had him holding his ears and gritting his teeth as tears ran down his cheeks.

The Keeper said, "Calm yourself and you will suffer no pain. It is always your choice, you see. Now, accept my authority. Remove your slippers and go to the set of three steps that you see in the center of the oval rug."

"Calm yourself," muttered Doctor Fayne. "Accept my authority, he says. Ah, what's the use. They've cooked my goose." He kicked off his slippers and shrugged.

When his feet touched the rug's softness, his intense expression shifted to a half-smile. As if in a hypnotic trance, he gazed at the gold velvet rug. Then, throwing himself on it, he rolled from side to side in a rocking motion.

The Keeper said, "I see you are reacting sensually to the gold velvet, Doctor. But this is not the appropriate time for such activity. Go to the first step now or you will be repelled from the rug with such force that your body will ricochet around this chamber like a ping-pong ball."

Moving slowly, the Doctor went to the first step. "Kneel on the first step and place your arms on the padded rail and look at the golden screen. Relax now. Yes, you are relaxing. Your mood is softening. You are less anxious now. The tranquilizers are taking effect. We will soon be able to begin our dialogue."

Doctor Fayne stared at the blurry golden circle in the center of the screen and heaved a heavy sigh. Then he said, "What's going on here? My last confession? Then down the aisle to my doom? Sentenced to eternal gloom?"

"We are not here to send you to your doom, Doctor Fayne. We are here to help you," replied The Keeper.

"We are not here to bury Caesar, but to praise him," replied the Doctor. "Next comes the blood bath."

"Cease the nonsense, Doctor. Calm yourself. Do not resist the tranquilizer effect. Easy now. Slow your thoughts. Cooperate with..."

Before the sentence ended, Doctor Fayne shouted, "Take your cooperation and shove it!" The room filled with an ear-splitting reverberation of the Doctor's voice and he experienced another cycle of pain. When it had subsided he moaned. "Deserted. Shafted. Abandoned. Where are you, God? Where have you been and where did you go?"

"Cease this inane babbling, Doctor Fayne," said The Keeper. "Why do you keep blaming others for your situation? You are at the root of your own problems. There is no need to appeal to your distant and invisible God. I am your Keeper. At this shelter, we are all here to help you. Do let us help you. Let go of your resistance. Comply. In compliance is your only contentment."

"Let go. Comply. Help. Let go..." Doctor Fayne's mood was softening as he calmed down considerably. A glazed look entered his eyes as the tranquilizers took effect.

"You are relaxing now, Doctor," said The Keeper. "Soon

your mind will rid itself of its mental clutter and you will be able to reflect rationally on your past. We will trace your life from its beginning to the present. The memory stimulator we have administered will give you remarkably clear recall as well as keen insights into your past actions. You will be able to reveal the deepest innermost truths about yourself. And this will help move you toward optimum health."

"Clutter. Memory. Truths. Health."

"Yes, health, Doctor Fayne. We call this process The Unveiling. We will remove the barriers that are keeping you out of touch with your true self. We will work together to come to an understanding of your baffling deviation from the acceptable norm. Then we will be in an excellent position to dispose of...uh...er...dispose of your case in a manner beneficial to The New Social System."

Doctor Fayne was silent now, staring at the blurry golden circle in the center of the golden screen-like translucent wall.

"We are about to begin, Doctor," said The Keeper. "We will burrow into the inner Fayne in search of your truth. I will guide you, and we will meet as often as my busy schedule permits. Be assured that we will persist."

The vertical crease in the center of the Doctor's forehead was smooth now. The pupils of his eyes were dilated. He was resting against the armrest of the escalating device on the steps, and kneeling in a fairly relaxed posture.

Slumping over the armrest, with his arms folded under his chin, Doctor Fayne seemed passive now, and receptive. His eyelids hung heavily and he seemed to be staring straight head without truly seeing anything.

"Tell me, Doctor Fayne, what is your first childhood memory?" asked The Keeper.

"The orphanage."

"How old were you?"

"About four."

"What do you remember about the orphanage?"

"There was a girl who was visiting me. Blonde. Blue-eyed. Young. In her teens, I think. Softness. That's what I remember. Softness and gentleness."

"Who was she?"

"I don't know. There were no girls at the Home. Only us boys and the Brothers who ran the place."

"Perhaps she was a volunteer."

"Maybe."

"Why do you think you remember her?"

"Her warmth. I could tell she cared about me. But then she was gone. Among the missing."

"What was the name of the orphanage?"

"The Home of the Holy Sepulchre. It was run by the Brothers of Taberna, a Catholic order of monks."

"Where was the orphanage located?"

"In the South Side of New Grafton."

"Were the Brothers kind to you?"

"Not very often. Most of the time they were cruel. We were whipped and beaten to keep us in line. There was a lot of crying at the Home. And lots of pain. The routine was work, study, punishment…in an endless cycle."

"Do endless cycles bother you, Doctor Fayne?"

"Yes. They bore me and irritate me. I enjoy doing new things, exploring new options. I like change."

"So the regularity of the orphanage stifled you?"

"Right."

"What about your family of origin, Doctor? Were you informed about that?"

"I was only told that I was left at the Home when I was an infant and my name was Wylie Fayne. The rest is a mystery. I stayed at the orphanage till I was nine years old and then..."

"Just a moment, Doctor. Let's move more slowly. Tell me how the orphanage affected you and how you felt about being an orphan."

"I felt abandoned. Trapped. Restless. Dissatisfied.

Frustrated. Lonely. I felt empty and lost. I felt very different from people around me. I felt like a person who had come here from another place in the universe and ended up on the wrong planet."

"Did you have any dreams or fantasies about things being otherwise?"

"Yes. I often had the idea that by some kind of miracle my parents would show up some day and set me free and we'd live happily ever after like the characters in a Dickens novel. But the dream didn't come true. So I tried to accept my status as an orphan. Yet there were always reminders. I envied anyone who had two parents, or even one."

"So you were lonely and dissatisfied and you were punished often by the Brothers. Describe life at the orphanage, Doctor."

"Their motto was 'Dedicated to the Salvation of Abandoned Boys.' The Brothers had a pretty harsh idea of what salvation was all about. If you disobeyed or broke a rule or even balked a little you got the horsewhip. One boy who tried to run away got beaten so fiercely they had to take him to the hospital. And he never came back. We heard rumors that he had died. So that was an example to us.

"Life at the orphanage was totally disciplined. The Brothers had a complete book publishing operation and every orphan was part of the enterprise. When I was only five years old I was working in the book bindery carrying glue pots to the cover machine. By the time I was seven I was running a cover machine. At nine I was an apprentice to a typesetter.

"I didn't know what being a child was. I only knew about work. Up at dawn every day. Scrubbing floors and cleaning up before breakfast. Oatmeal for breakfast. Daily Mass in the chapel. School. A light lunch. Working in the bindery. Religious instruction. Memorizing prayers. Singing hymns. A skimpy piece of meat and bland vegetables for supper.

Evening Benediction. Assigned reading. Baths. Sleep. Day after day. On and on. The same pattern.

"On Sundays there were visitors. And the volunteers came to help us get our chores done early. That's when she came. Now I remember about the blonde girl. She was a Taberna volunteer and her name was Iris. Warm, beautiful Iris. She wasn't visiting me for very long. Soon she was gone. But over the years she has come to me often in my dreams." The Doctor stopped and began to smile warmly at the memory of Iris. Then he heaved a large sigh and began shaking his head.

The Keeper asked, "Who else gave you affection at the Home?"

The deviant paused for a few moments. "Brother Favian. Yes, he was kind. He used to wink at the regulations sometimes. And he'd take a few of us aside and tell us about the outside world. He let me read books that weren't on our assigned reading list. *David Copperfield. Les Miserables. The Count of Monte Cristo. Gulliver's Travels.* He advised me to chase after knowledge on my own.

"Brother Favian was gentle and friendly and I grew attached to him. He was like a substitute father for me. But when I was eight years old they transferred him. I can still remember the black mood I sunk into after he went to an assignment in another Province. That's when I began to plan my escape from the Home. I knew there wasn't much hope of escaping. And I realized my brown uniform would give me away. But I had to try.

"I chose a Sunday when the visitors and volunteers would be there. I thought I could blend in with the visitors when they were leaving. But there, waiting at the gate, stood Brother Victor, the dean of discipline. He was built like a truck and if you crossed him up you'd regret it. A very heavy feeling came over me when I saw him. A feeling of futility. I remembered the boy who tried to run away. Brother Victor had whipped him with all of us watching, to teach us a lesson.

"So I knew it was no use. I stopped in my tracks, gave up hope, and became very quiet. I began spending more time in the chapel, turning to God for the strength to accept my fate. And when I was about nine, Mrs. Turnbull came to the orphanage looking for three boys and..."

"Wait just a moment," said The Keeper. "You mentioned turning to God for assistance. What did this consist of?"

"Bible reading. Stations of the Cross. Novenas. All kinds of prayers. Doing extra things to bring me closer to God. What else could I do? Where could I turn? I was angry with God for making me an orphan. But I learned, little by little, to accept my situation as part of His plan for me instead of as a punishment. 'The Imitation of Christ' helped me a lot: 'He who can suffer best will have most peace, and who is the true conqueror of himself is the true lord of the world.'

"In my nine-year-old mind it was hard for me to look at suffering as a good thing. But Kempis' writing helped. I could see that his writing applied to me. Likewise with the New Testament: 'He who does not take up his Cross and follow me is not worthy of me.' 'The stone which the builders rejected has become...'"

The Keeper interrupted. "I see your point. You have given enough examples about your religious inclinations. Now, what about Mrs. Turnbull? You were saying that she came looking for three boys when you were about nine."

The deviant's voice was calm and steady now. The tranquilizers were working very well. There was no evident paranoia. No rage. "Grace Turnbull was a very strong-minded woman. She was a widow with white hair and a purple face that matched her fierce temper. And she was as strong as any three men together. She always kept five or six orphans as wards. Her only income was what she got from the Province for our care. When her wards were old enough they would leave and she'd get some new ones to replace them. We were the new ones that year.

"She had rules about everything and if you broke one you might find her fist hitting your face so hard you'd fly across the room and bounce off the wall. So you'd learn to keep her rules. She had a punishment for every crime. She put us alone in dark cellars and attics to reflect on our wrongdoings. If she caught two of us breaking a rule she'd crack our heads together till we saw stars. If you swore, she would stuff your mouth with liquid lye soap and make you gargle it until you gagged on it.

"For talking back, we'd have to eat strong horseradish. If she caught you smoking, she'd shove a lit cigarette up your nose, clamp her hand over your mouth, and make you inhale until your eyes were red with tears and you'd be coughing so hard you thought you were dying. For outright disobedience she whipped us on our legs with a studded leather belt. She also used stiff hairbrushes on our rear ends. And sometimes she would give you a sting by flicking the end of a wet dishtowel at you if you didn't concentrate well enough while washing the dishes.

"Her punishments were always related to our crimes. If she caught one of us masturbating she'd force us to simulate masturbation with a rough cloth rubbing against our penises until they were red and raw. Then she'd pour a mixture of alcohol and water on the rawness and the pain was beyond description. We'd crouch like sleeping cats for hours, and we'd remember the punishment for a long time. She was strict and she was cruel. There was no question about who was in charge."

"How did you feel about her behavior?" asked The Keeper.

"Frustrated and angry. But there was respect, too. She went out of her way to be fair and there were no favorites in her house. Brother Victor was that way at the Home. Even though you hated him for what he was doing, you respected his sense of impartial justice. And as I grew older at Mrs. Turnbull's the punishment lessened and we mainly got lectures and confinement to our rooms. As time went by I feared her less and respected her more.

"She was intelligent in an earthy way. And we had a common bond. She had lost her husband. We boys had lost our parents. 'You got to get the education to make a go of things,' she'd insist. 'It's no easy road startin' out as an orphan with nothing but your name to call your own,' she would say. She was always motivating us to think for ourselves and make something of ourselves. 'It's every man for himself in this world, and the devil take the hindmost,' she repeated often. The older I got the more I understood her and got along with her."

"When things were bad there, did you ever think of running away?"

"Of course. But what was the use? We were told that anyone who had ever tried it ended up back at the orphanage. So none of us tried to run away. After all, even though she was strict we had a lot of freedom compared to living within the walls of the Home. The food was much better. She was a good cook. And even though she kept us busy, we boys had some fun together.

"We all had part-time jobs. I delivered newspapers when I was ten. When I was twelve I washed dishes in a restaurant. Later I did short-order cooking. We turned in what we earned and she took some for the household and used the rest on clothes for us. For orphans, we were very well dressed. She taught us to be proud of our appearance and never to be passive in the face of tough times.

"'The good Lord helps those that help themselves,' she'd say. She always pushed us to make our own way and she never took a cent of charity. She was proud of that. She was independent and very religious. A very strict Catholic. We all went to Sunday School every week. And there were group prayers at home, too. Her pride was contagious. She was an excellent teacher. A motivator. She pushed us hard to make good grades so we'd be eligible for college scholarships."

"Your attitude about her has shifted from anger to admiration," said The Keeper. "Explain that."

"It's simple. I understood her good and bad aspects, that's all. Even when she was cruel I knew there were good reasons behind what she was doing. I learned to be grateful for her training. So did the other boys. Her training helped us tremendously in later years."

"How did you relate to other boys in your early years, Doctor?"

"At the orphanage, close friendships were discouraged. They didn't want any rebellions on their hands. But at Mrs.Turnbull's I was very close to the boys who were my age, especially the Petrell twins, Noah and Sloan. We were together during the last couple of years of elementary school and right on through most of high school. Then they went to live with their aunt and uncle."

"How did you react to their departure?"

"I was dejected. I felt deserted. I was depressed. But then I made friends with Frankie Shagg. He lived in another foster home in the same neighborhood near Mrs. Turnbull. He was tough and wouldn't take any abuse from anybody. I learned a lot from Frankie. He wasn't much for studying but he was good at survival. We shared a lot of sarcasm and off-color humor together. And I think that helped me get a lot of my adolescent frustrations out of my system."

"Did you have sexual frustrations at that time?"

"Doesn't every adolescent? But Mrs. Turnbull kept reminding us about the risks of getting involved with girls. She made it clear that if we wanted to get ahead we'd have to avoid close relationships with girls. 'There'll be plenty of time for the girlies later,' she'd warn us. So, even though we went to dances and walked girls home, we'd never bring one to Mrs. Turnbull's place."

"You had no sexual intimacy with girls?"

"No. I concentrated on my education."

"Did you have sexual intimacy with boys?"

"No."

"Tell me about your education, Doctor."

"I studied liberal arts at Avernus Catholic College, staying with Mrs. Turnbull during my first two years. But after my second year Mrs. Turnbull died. Then I found a room for myself near the college."

"Did you distinguish yourself at Avernus Catholic?"

"I was an honors student, editor of our weekly newspaper, Student Council President, and member of the debating society."

"What was your major field of study within the liberal arts?"

"At first it was history; then I became more interested in philosophy, psychology and theology. So I changed my major to philosophy."

"After graduating, what was your next step?"

"I decided I needed a break from the academic routine. My night job as a typesetter was paying me good money. So I started working the day shift and spent my spare time having fun. I concentrated on drinking and dating and becoming more worldly. And the more worldly I became, the less spiritual I was. God could wait. I had other things to do. I hung around with hard-drinking war veterans who introduced me to the world of gambling, and I was an eager student of their way of life.

"I made the rounds of the race tracks and casinos, always with a pretty girl on my arm, and I worked at being sophisticated. I was as dedicated to fun as I had been to studying. Instead of restraining my appetites I fed them. And they grew. The more I indulged myself the more I craved higher levels of self-indulgence. Then the boredom of it all hit me! I remembered the old Wylie Fayne with his discipline and self-fulfillment. So I started thinking about going on for a Master of Arts in philosophy, and maybe a doctorate later. Teaching at the university level began to appeal to me. I figured it would be a satisfying life.

"So I went back to Avernus Catholic and buckled down to an academic way of life. My choice was the right one. The deeper I got into theology, psychology and philosophy the more I was fascinated by it. And I knew there was more material available than anyone person could ever master. That suited me.

"I've always thrived on challenges. Easy pursuits held no interest for me. Mind-bending subjects were the ones I had to pursue. I enjoyed teaching difficult subjects, too. I received a teaching fellowship in the Graduate School at Avernus Catholic. So, with the help of the teaching fellowship, I was able to reduce my work week as a typesetter to part-time and finance my own way through graduate school."

"Did you eventually receive your doctorate in philosophy?"

"Yes."

"Did you then begin teaching full-time at the college?"

"No. Toward the end of my studies I began to wonder if I might have a religious vocation. So right after receiving my Ph.D. I decided to spend some time in a monastery to sort things through. Avernus Catholic was cooperative and said there would be a position waiting for me if I made the decision to return to teaching. Then I went to the mountains of...to the...to the mountains...to the mountains of..."

The deviant straightened up from his slumped posture and the glazed look began to leave his eyes. Then the vertical crease in his forehead deepened. "Go on, Doctor," said The Keeper. "Continue."

"Pater et filius et spiritus sanctus. The Father and the Son and the Holy Ghost. Spiritus sanctus. Spiritus sanc.."

"Enough," ordered The Keeper. "Cease this shift from a living tongue to a dead one. Is this use of Latin a device to avoid the truth?"

Doctor Fayne stared at the blurry golden circle in the center of the golden screen. "The truth has fled the scene of the crime. The truth has no truck with these times. Where oh where has my little truth gone? Where oh where can it be? Where oh where has my..."

"Control yourself," ordered The Keeper. "Cooperate. We want to restore you to health. Trust us. We are very concerned about you, Doctor Fayne."

"Concerned? Hah!" The deviant shook his head. "Trust you? Like the fly trusted the spider? Come into my parlor, said the spider to the fly. Trust you? Oh boy!"

"Let us continue our dialogue," said The Keeper. "When we are done with The Unveiling you will be a healthy member of The New Social System. Carry on where you left off, please."

"Carrion? Carry on? Quoth the raven, nevermore! To be or not to be is not the question. It is the answer. The question is what does a raven quoth. And why doth a spider ingest a fly? Why does it carry on that way?"

"Enough," ordered The Keeper. "The drugs must be wearing off. Or they are having a paradoxical effect on our deviant. I believe our session is over, Doctor."

The deviant returned to his slumped posture on the kneeler, allowing his head to rest on his folded arms. Then, in a monotone, he recited from Francis Thompson's poem: "I fled Him, down the nights and down the days. I fled Him, down the arches of the years. I fled Him, down the labyrinthine ways of my own mind, and in the midst of tears I hid from Him, and under..."

"Stop this idle babbling and return to your triangle," said The Keeper. "I have no time to listen to you babble on."

"Babylon? Babylon, oh Babylon, let's travel on...to Babylon. 'Across the margent of the world I fled, and troubled the gold gateways of the stars, smiting for shelter on their clanged bars. Fretted to...'"

"Cease the versifying, Doctor. It can be very irritating. I will call Sumner now and he will return you to your triangle," said The Keeper. "Rise now or you will trigger an electrifying impulse that will jolt you into compliance."

"Electrify? Electric eye? Electric guy? Elect a fly? Hah! Oh boy, I wonder if...Hrgh! Argh!" The deviant was thrown into a convulsion by the jolt of power. His eyes bugged out and his mouth was open wide with consternation.

When his tremors diminished, The Keeper asked, "Are you now ready to return to your triangle, Doctor Fayne?"

"Return?"

"Yes, return."

"Yes."

After being ordered to put on his slippers, and told not to linger on the velvet rug, he complied with the orders. This was followed by a click and a buzz and a hum. Then the door slid open and The Keeper said, "Go into the corridor now and rejoin Sumner. Go to your triangle, Doctor, and rest."

"Rest," replied the deviant. "Yes, rest. Rest in peace."

Case Report Disposition: Observation to be continued.

3

Case Report
Deviant: Fayne, Wylie, Ph.D.
Number: 1
Shelter: Bentham Deviant Shelter
Province: Avernus
Housing: Total Scrutiny
Therapy: Time Void
Technique: Observation and Dialogue
Condition: To be ascertained

Summary of Session Number 3

When I made my next observation, the deviant was in one of his very orderly phases. Sitting with perfect posture at his word processor, he was repeatedly typing the phrase, "Cleanliness is next to godliness." Each line of words was letter perfect. His typing, his appearance, and his triangle were all in a state of extreme neatness.

Rising from his word processor, he smoothed out his smock and went to his bookcase. He chose a red-covered book with a black rectangle on the cover. The title was *Summa Theologica*. Looking at the book, he said, "Well, Professor Aquinas, what will we talk about today?"

Shuffling to the scoop-back chair, he cupped the book in his left hand, carefully opened it, then leafed through the pages. "Yes, here is the section on the Union of Body and Soul. This is where Aquinas discusses the natural philosophers and their thoughts on primary matter." He looked up at the nearest camera. "Today we will discuss the..."

Stopping in mid-sentence, he turned the book over and said with a smile, "Why, it is you, Urda," A silvery spider was on his left index finger. "How good of you to stop by for a visit." Shifting the book to his right hand, he held the finger with the spider on it near his eyes and asked, "Where have you been, Urda? I was wondering about your state of health. I have been asking your ant friend, Verdandi, and your flea friend, Skuld, if they knew where you were. But I got no clear answer from them.

"If I had decided not to read Aquinas, you would still be among the missing. Have I infringed on your privacy? Were you meditating? Weaving an eternal web? Contemplating the One, the True, and the Good? There is no need to reply. You have a right to your own habits. But I must do my program now, Urda. The camera is operating. So I will return you to the bookcase where you may continue what you were doing."

As he went to the bookcase with Urda, he said, "One of you always seems to be among the missing. Where does a spider amble in a hermitage such as this one? And where does an ant scurry? And a flea leap? You need not respond. It is well for all creatures to have a place where they may retire from the busyness of daily life, as I have done. It is only my concern for your welfare that stirs my curiosity. Forgive me for prying."

At the bookcase, Doctor Fayne took the hand with the spider on it, placed it slowly into the space where the Aquinas volume had been, and waited patiently as the spider moved along his knuckles and onto the nearby book titled *Humanistic Poetry*. Then the Doctor smiled and said, "There now. You are back where you wanted to be. Safe and sound."

RESEARCH NOTE
The terms used by the deviant indicate that he was referring to three figures found in Norse mythology. The Norns last appeared in literature as the three weird sisters in Shakespeare's Macbeth. Doctor Fayne's Urda, the spider, represents the Past. Verdandi, the ant, symbolizes the

Present. And Skuld, the flea, stands for the Future.

Experts on mythology say that the Norns guarded Urda's Well, where the gods came every day, after passing over a rainbow bridge. Sitting beside the well, they passed judgment on the deeds of men. Another view of the Norns is that they are similar to the three Fates of Greek mythology. Descended from the giants, the Norns are described as old women who feed the roots of the World-Tree and preside over men's destinies. I believe that sufficiently explains Doctor Fayne's references.

After returning the spider to its place of refuge, the deviant went back to his book, seated himself carefully, and in a stage voice he looked directly at the video camera and said, "Now let us begin today's discussion on the relationship between body and soul. Thomas Aquinas, by the way, was a thirteenth century philosopher who was raised to sainthood. His writings were landmarks in the development of Christian thought. He was not fond of Plato and primarily utilized the thinking of Aristotle, who was Plato's prize pupil.

"Aquinas made it clear that the only meaningful philosophy was one that looked on man as a composite being with body and soul working together toward one end...union with God. Aquinas is credited with restoring the balance between idea and reality, you see."

Pausing with a half-smile on his face, Doctor Fayne bowed his head three times as if acknowledging applause. Then he returned to the book discussion. "According to Aquinas, we cannot function on the sense level, as brutes, and be true human beings. Nor can we function only in the highest planes of the intellect as if we had no bodies. We function as a blend of higher and lower functions. We thank God for both body and soul. Now, after a brief pause for a message of interest to all of you, we will return with more..."

Closing the book, the deviant placed it on the utility table, sat back in his scoop-back chair, and gazed steadily at the black velvet wall. His eyelids began to droop, a half-smile came onto his face, and he said very softly, "Iris? Is it you? I did not realize your hair was so long and so very blonde. You look so well. Thank you for dropping by to see me. I have very little company here in my hermitage. But, as you know, my isolation is completely voluntary. I need to be alone to dwell on the truths of existence, you see. I have chosen this life of solitude to contemplate and move into closer union with God, my dear."

He nodded his head twice, as if listening to a voice. Then he said, "Yes, Iris, I am well aware of your beauty and your goodness. They are radiant qualities in you and light up the world around you. You are a pleasure to see and to hear. Am I content, you ask? How could I be more content, Iris? I have my word processor and my solitude and my basic necessities. What more do I need? Less is better, my dear. Less is always better.

"My distractions are at a minimum. And my three women respect my privacy as I respect theirs. What did you say about the three women? No, my dear, you must not think such thoughts. My relationship with Urda, Verdandi, and Skuld is strictly platonic, if Aquinas will pardon my use of Plato's name. You see, Aquinas was very critical of Plato. And the word 'platonic' derives from Plato's name. Forgive my digression, Iris. I enjoy playing with words. What have you been doing with yourself since your last visit to see me?"

Doctor Fayne was silent for a few moments. "Apparently, you want me to explain my three women companions, Iris. Well, Urda is a silvery spider, Verdandi is a red ant, and Skuld is a dark brown flea. The three of them share my hermitage. What do we have in common? Our environment and our lives. But we are worlds apart when it comes to time. Each of them leans heavily toward the past, present or future. And I have been learning to free myself of all three phases of time. This puts me in touch with eternity, where I am most fully myself."

The deviant's glazed eyes were fixed on the black velvet wall as he nodded. "Yes, Iris, I am aware that you are no longer within the boundaries of time. No, I do not expect you to fully explain it to me. Yes, I understand that a person must be one with it to understand it. Yes, I look forward to joining you there, when God is willing. But I still have work to do here. I have my books and my writing and my meditation and teaching to do. Yes, I know it is a solitary mission. But I have always tended toward being a solitary person. It is no major sacrifice for me. It is a labor of love. And it brings me closer to...Iris? Gone. She arrives quickly, without notice. Then she leaves quickly, also without notice. May God watch over you constantly, Iris. Thank you for dropping by."

Heaving a deep sigh, his head hung down so that his bearded chin touched his chest. With closed eyes, he prayed for God to be with Iris and with him, too. Then he took a leather-bound book titled *Blessed Be God* and opened it at random. "What an interesting coincidence," he said. "We have a quote from Aquinas here: 'The cross is my sure salvation; the cross I ever adore... '"

Flipping the book open at random another time, he began repeating, "Inviolata." Then he repeated a particular phrase from the prayer several times. "'...that our minds and bodies may be pure...that our minds and bodies may be pure...'"

He got up and went to the washbowl and, while muttering "Inviolata," he washed his hands with liquid soap many times. While he was doing this, a click and a buzz indicated that the sliding door of his triangle was about to open. He continued to rub his hands under the blow-drier as Sumner entered the room.

Sumner muttered, "Looks like he's having one of his clean fits. There's nothing for me to clean up. Hey, Fayne, what are you doing? Cleaning the skin right off your hands?"

"Oh, it's you, Brother Summoner. It's difficult to hear you with the drier blowing. Cleanliness is next to Godliness, you see."

"I am not your brother Summoner, Fayne. I'm Sumner, understand? And I'm your attendant, not your brother." He addressed the Doctor. "The Kuh...Kuh...Keeper wants to see you in his chamber, so let's get moving."

Doctor Fayne smiled. "Do you mean to say that Father Abbot wishes to see me, Brother Summoner? Well, I will be right with you." He went slowly to his utility table, took his prayer book and the volume of Aquinas, returned them to the bookcase, and kneeled while peering into the bookcase and saying, "Are you comfortable, Urda? Yes, I see you now. I will be gone for a while, visiting Father Abbot. But I expect to return soon. If you see Verdandi and Skuld, please let them know where I am. Peace be with you, Urda."

"Enough of that loony talk, Fayne," said Sumner. "Nobody keeps the Kuh...Kuh...Keeper waiting."

"Father Abbot is patient, Brother Summoner, as you will learn to be after you have been in the monastery a while."

"This isn't a monastery, Fayne." He waved his hand toward the sliding door which immediately opened. "This is a Psycho Deviant Shelter."

Sumner followed the deviant into the corridor and Doctor Fayne said, "You may call it what you wish, but a monastery by any other name is still a monastery. You may call me any name you wish, too, but in the final analysis I am simply Brother Wylie, a member of The Order of the Holy Chalice."

"Ah, you're way over the border, Fayne. One time I come in and you're wild and raunchy and another time you're some kind of religious fanatic. I don't know why I even bother talking to you."

The Doctor remained silent as they walked along the corridor. Then there was a slight tremor and the sound of distant rumbling. "Probably some of those FRN sympathizers planting their bombs. Or maybe another one of those demonstrations with fireworks about that writer Lance Crowne. They want that traitor dead, Fayne. I don't think they'd be satisfied if he went to a patho shelter for retraining or reorganizing his brain. No. They want him dead."

"Violence. Death. Fear. War," said the Doctor in a stage voice. "It is the history of the human race, resulting from lust for power and possessions instead of love of God and others." He then recited the Lord's Prayer.

Sumner said, "You're so screwed up, Fayne."

"You are entitled to your perspective."

Doctor Fayne was compliant during his time in The Clean Room, preparing to see The Keeper. He kept muttering, "Cleanliness is next to Godliness."

In The Keeper's chamber, after the deviant received doses of tranquilizer and memory stimulator, The Keeper said, "Time is of the essence, Doctor Fayne. Go to the edge of the oval golden velvet rug and remove your slippers, leaving them on the floor."

The Doctor bowed his head reverently, looking at the set of three steps in the middle of the rug. "Yes, this must be the confessional."

"Quite otherwise, Doctor Fayne. This is my chamber which is not part of a religious institution. Now remove your slippers and proceed to the first step where you will remain in place with your arms on the armrest and your gaze focused on the golden screen. Proceed. You have my permission."

The Doctor nodded his head politely, made the Sign of the Cross as he stepped onto the rug, said, "Lead us not into temptation" and muttered several times, "Deliver us from evil." When he was in position on the first step, his face seemed peaceful.

The Keeper said, "Remember that I am concerned about

you, Doctor Fayne, and I am here to help you."

"Father Abbot, there is no need to be concerned. I am quite content here in the monastery."

"This is not a monastery, Doctor. It is the Bentham Psychological Deviant Shelter. Your egocentric religious tangent will shift in a moment. Then we will begin our therapeutic dialogue. For now, just relax."

When the medications took effect, The Keeper reviewed where they had left off in their previous discussion. "...so now let us talk about your time in the monastery. Try to gather your thoughts in a logical sequence as we continue our quest for truth. We must cure you of your deviation, Doctor Fayne. Remain where you are on the first step. And do not move to the second or third step without my permission."

His eyes were glazed now. "Yes, I understand. It will be as you wish."

"Continue, please. Explain your time in the monastery."

"I had gone on retreats to The Mount of the Holy Chalice and the thought entered my mind that I needed a long time of reflection after my intense years of study. I knew I was at an important transition period in my life and wanted to come to terms with who I was, put my life in perspective, and map out some goals. So I got permission to remain there for a year without taking any vows.

"There was a shelter for the homeless about halfway down the mountain and they let me stay there as a visitor. I could join the Brothers in their services and live as much like a monk as I wished, yet I still had freedom of movement. It was an ideal arrangement."

"Did you consider staying at the monastery on a permanent basis?"

"No, I knew that a year would be enough."

"And you stayed the full year?"

"Yes."

"What did you accomplish by going there?"

"I became more disciplined spiritually. I increased my self-awareness. I improved my conscious contact with my Creator. I truly got in touch with my own spirit. It was a very worthwhile year. I went back to my career at the college with enthusiasm and a fresh outlook. I had a clear mind and a peaceful heart."

"At the monastery, did you come to terms with your orphaned status and your time in the orphanage?"

"I came to terms with everything in my life, including the Church. I was able to review the events of my life, make sense out of the chaos of my early years, and see myself clearly for the first time. I also could see the need to become less of a perfectionist and I made a pledge to myself to be more realistic, more practical, more accepting."

"I see. Back at Avernus Catholic, did you now find a balanced existence as a professor of philosophy?"

"Yes."

"You have said nothing about sexual activity, Doctor. Were you not intimate with anyone during this period of your life?"

"I just had ordinary friendships. No deeply intimate relationships."

"Was this based on fear or on a rational decision to remain free of entanglements?"

"Maybe it involved a little of both. My career came first. And after my experiences with women during my fling at being worldly, I had some reservations about the effect women had on me. They could throw me off balance."

"Explain, please."

"Well, I'd get so preoccupied with them and so sensitive, it was almost like catching a virus and having fevers. The intensity was very unnerving. I found that I was better off keeping my friendships with women on the light side."

"Did you have the ordinary natural attraction to the

opposite sex?"

"Yes. In fact, that was the problem. The attraction was very powerful. When I got too interested in a woman I could feel myself losing control and I didn't like that feeling. Besides, I figured 35 would be a good age to get married. So, I avoided women who seemed bent on going to the altar and I kept myself single."

"At age 30, were you comfortably settled at Avernus Catholic while teaching philosophy?"

"Yes. I was doing very well. I had been advanced to associate professor and was in line for the department chair. I'd found a wonderful mentor in Mark Hiller, who was nearing retirement. He shared my interest in medieval and ancient thought and we also became close friends.

"Mark was the first non-Jesuit to chair the Philosophy Department at Avernus Catholic. When I was 32, he arranged to move me to full professor. And when I was 34 I followed in his path. I became the youngest philosophy chairperson in the history of the college. It was a very satisfying time for me. I felt appreciated and was able to cut back on my teaching load, do more independent study, and start my own philosophical newsletter, *The Journal of Ancient Wisdom.*

"It seemed as if everything was converging that year. My professional career was jelling. My income was secure. My personal relationships were satisfying. I had a fine apartment a short distance from the college. And I guess I was ready for Anna when she showed up in my class on Medieval Thought. When I looked at the class the first day and saw that beautiful innocent face in the first row, I felt as if I'd known her for a lifetime. I knew Anna Malone would be more than just another student.

"She was at the end of her studies for a master's degree in social work and took my course as an unrelated subject to round out her schedule. Her impact on me was tremendous.

She lit up the classroom with her beauty. When I was lecturing, my eyes would go to her automatically. It was a very powerful mutual attraction. At the end of class she'd always find a reason to come up and ask a question. Then we'd end up walking out of the building together. And one thing led to another."

"You became sexually involved with her?"

"Not right away. She was very sensitive about sex. She'd been physically abused in childhood. So she was cautious. We proceeded slowly. And that was fine with me. I didn't like pressure from women. I appreciated restraint. She had a lot of that quality so this gave us plenty of time to get to know each other."

"Did you find that you had much in common?"

"We had similarities and differences. She came from an upper class setting and led a fairly pampered childhood. But she was an orphan, too. She'd lost her parents in a fire when she was young and was raised by a wealthy old maid aunt. So we shared the same abandonment feelings and emotionally we were like twins. We shared the same religious background, too. We had a way of reading each other's thoughts and finishing each other's sentences. It was amazing how we related to each other. What a ray of sunshine she was."

"Describe her, please."

"She was a grownup version of Iris, the girl in my dreams. She had the same strawberry blonde hair and deep blue eyes, fair complexion, soft voice and very feminine mannerisms. Like the way she used her hands when she talked. And her voice entranced me so much that I'd actually forget what she was saying sometimes because I was caught up in the sound of her voice. I found her completely fascinating. And I guess I had the same effect on her. In no time we were inseparable."

"And you married her?"

"Yes. Within a few months after meeting her we became engaged and about a year after she got her social worker credentials we were married. We pooled our resources and bought a house with an office attached for her counseling and therapy practice. In the main house I had a library/office combination. And we each had our own bedroom. We were accustomed to privacy.

"Life seemed to be falling right into place. I was Chairman of the Philosophy Department and she became an independent clinical social worker. We were fulfilled professionally and personally. It was a meeting of minds and hearts. She became more interested in philosophy and I developed more interest in psychotherapy. And we had similar views about the moral decline of society."

"You had great respect for each other."

"That's an understatement."

"What about children? Did you have any?"

"No. She had a reproductive problem. There was a possibility of remedying it. But she was concerned about her ability to care for a child. So, we agreed to go on as we were, concentrating on each other and our professional lives."

"Did that frustrate you?"

"No. Life was satisfying to me as it was. Besides, I didn't see how I could fit a child into my life."

"So life was well balanced for you at this time?"

"Yes. And I began to get more and more recognition in my field. My *Journal* had a lot to do with it. The subscription list was steadily expanding. And I got more and more speaking engagements because I was striking a chord about the need to recall older values. It seemed as though I was linking medieval philosophy to modern times in a way that hadn't been done effectively by others. I guess my thinking provided a kind of bridge for people to cross over. I was making thought connections that were basically logical for me but hadn't entered a lot of other people's minds.

"So I found myself moving in high circles, not only in New Grafton but around the Province and in other provinces, too. I was invited to give after-dinner talks at banquets. I became a popular guest on radio and television talk shows. I was asked to serve on boards of directors of human service organizations. I was an integral part of the community, for the first time in my life. Yes, I was almost at peace with myself. Almost at peace."

"Why do you qualify that phrase, Doctor, by saying 'almost'?"

"Well, at the very time when things were beginning to go well for me I found myself developing more of a taste for whiskey. I can't really pin down how it began. I had always been fairly moderate up till then. Except for the time when I was on the race track circuit. But that was really just a fling to break the tension. And later I had made up my mind to be disciplined about my drinking.

"Anna and I used alcohol to relax us before making love. And I began to use it to ease the pressure of high visibility in public life. Also, I guess I used it to get some relief from my self-imposed discipline which could be pretty extreme. All I can say is that as time went by my bourbon became a more important part of my life."

"Would you say that you were becoming an alcoholic?"

"I didn't drink every day. I figured I could take it or leave it. So, it would have been hard for me to look at myself as an alcoholic. But I was becoming more dependent on it as a sedative. I can see now that it affected my moods. And that had an effect on my viewpoints. It was strange how my attitudes began to change at the very time when everything in life was coming together. I'm not sure how much the drinking entered into it and how much was clear thinking about the awful changes in society.

"I was accustomed to institutions that changed slowly. They had a solid foundation to them and weren't blown around by the winds of chance. But our society entered a transition period I wasn't prepared for psychologically. I wasn't a believer in change just for the sake of change. I was in favor of natural change, not radical change. But I began to feel that I was in a period of upheaval much more threatening than the Great Depression, the Second World War, and the prolonged Period of Planned International Tension.

"When the Period of Radical Change arrived I was out of step with it. It seemed as if change was being raised to the status of divinity. In fact, it was replacing divinity. Nothing was secure from it anymore. Not even the Church. Not even belief in God. Actually, there was widespread denial of God's existence. To me, for a person to deny God's existence made about as much sense as a fish denying the existence of water.

"Along with the decline of religion, there was a major decline in ethical standards. Instead of 'The end does not justify the means,' the ethical mood of the times indicated that any method could be justified in the pursuit of ambitious goals. This went against all of my basic values. Also, as a student of philosophy and history I knew that once they were in power the radical protesters would create new abuses to replace the ones they were claiming to erase. The notion that power corrupts is such an ancient piece of wisdom.

"The structure of society changed constantly. There was no keeping up with it. Government increased its power everywhere. At first, the Constitution was given lip service, then it was abolished. The private sector disappeared. Government took over all communication, food, fuel, energy and healthcare. The military was transformed into a national security force and defense was deemphasized.

"Every function was controlled by government which rationed all products and dictated all prices. Inflation reduced much of the population to the poverty level and turned people into wards of the state. When the radicals took power it was total. No half measures. Government by edict and executive order. Parliament was disbanded. Voting was no longer used to give citizens a voice. The only voice was the voice of the Econocracy with its usually nameless leaders.

"As the radicals rapidly changed society to fit their own utopian ideals, they also ridiculed and overturned the ancient values. Everything became relative, even God! There was no true Commandment. 'Grow Beyond Your Parents' replaced 'Honor Your Father and Mother.' The words 'Thou Shalt Not Commit Adultery' became 'Enjoy Being Sexually Active With Any Consenting Adult of either Sex.' The words 'Thou shalt not covet' were replaced by the claim 'More Is Better!'"

The Keeper interrupted him. "What happened with your Catholic ideas prior to the time when we abolished religion?"

"I held to my religious principles while the Church started to change its basic values. It remained silent in the face of governmental pressure. No longer did it stress the Seven Deadly Sins. Nor The Cardinal Virtues. In the Period of Radical Change the deadly sins had become goals of living.

"How could anyone condemn pride, lust, anger, greed, gluttony, envy and sloth? The economy thrived on satisfying them. And the virtues of prudence, justice, temperance and fortitude were loosely interpreted or ridiculed. Pretty soon the Church was looking at its own practices as relics of ancient times in need of change. No longer was there any respect for symbolism and mysticism. Not in the Period of Radical Change.

"When the changes hit Avernus Catholic College, it was like a tidal wave that nobody could stop. First, the government-sponsored radicals took a majority on the board of trustees. Then they changed the charter to make the college secular instead of religious. They relegated the Jesuits to a state of irrelevance. And finally, they changed the name from Avernus Catholic College to Avernus

University. It all seemed to happen overnight the way it was happening with other institutions. It had reached the point where if your bank or restaurant had a new name you hardly even noticed it.

"At the University they did it all with brief memos explaining each new change. No room for questioning. No voice on the part of faculty. No democratic process. No room for criticism. And even though I became more and more irritated by what was going on, I tried to accept things. But my resentment built to a point where I knew I had to take a stand. Although Anna advised against it, I went ahead and used my *Journal* to do it.

"I criticized the radical changes and argued for holding onto traditional ways and utilizing the wisdom of other times. But they called me an eccentric, a throwback to another era. My campaign for moderation made me look like a radical reactionary. In a paradoxical way, by confronting the radicalism I began to look like a radical in my own right. This got under my skin. My aim in life wasn't to be a radical. I believed in cooperation and harmony. But my beliefs were being tested now, at work and at home."

The Keeper asked, "How were they being tested?"

"I was caught between my desire for friendship and love and my need to be true to myself. So, I lost friends at the university and became more isolated. At home I began to see Anna pulling away from me gradually. I wondered what was happening to me and asked myself critical questions. Was my own attitude the problem? Or was it only natural for me to react? Was I reaching a professional burnout stage? Or was I just thinking clearly as I watched the world around me deteriorating? I began losing confidence in my own...I began losing...I began losing confidence in...I began losing..."

"Stay with our dialogue, Doctor," said The Keeper. "You are doing fine. The Unveiling is coming along quite nicely. Calm yourself. Gain control of your thoughts."

"Gain control...yes...control. I could feel that I was losing control. Losing confidence. Losing..."

"Enough, Doctor Fayne. The medication is apparently wearing off. And time is of the essence. If you must babble on, do it in your own triangle. Go now, please. Rejoin Sumner in the corridor and he will lead you back to your place."

"Yes, Father Abbot," said the Doctor. "I will join Brother Summoner." He made the Sign of The Cross. "In the name of the Father, and of the Son, and of the Holy Ghost. Amen."

Stepping onto the gold velvet rug, it was apparent that he was sensually stimulated. "Lead us not into temptation," he muttered, repeating the Sign of The Cross several times.

"Go to your slippers and put them on, Doctor."

"Yes, Father Abbot."

Doctor Fayne's face was peaceful as he put on his slippers. Then suddenly he threw himself onto his knees on the hard metallic floor. Holding the palms of his hands together in prayer posture, he looked upward and said, "Thank you, Lord, for all the blessings you have bestowed on me."

"Rise, Doctor," urged The Keeper. "This is not a chapel. All chapels and churches have been destroyed. This is the Psychological Deviant Shelter in Bentham. Go now."

"Yes, Father Abbot. In obedience, I will return to my hermitage now. Thank you, Father Abbot. May God bless you. And please pray for me."

The Keeper's voice was showing frustration. "Go, Doctor. Go to your triangle now...and rest."

Doctor Fayne shuffled toward the door and muttered, "Yes, rest. Rest in peace."

Case Report Disposition
Observation to be continued.

4

Case Report
Deviant: Fayne, Wylie, Ph.D.
Number: 1
Shelter: Bentham Deviant Shelter
Province: Avernus
Housing: Total Scrutiny
Therapy: Time Void
Technique: Observation and Dialogue
Condition: To be ascertained.

<u>Summary of Session Number 4</u>

The deviant was quite agitated when I made my next observation. He huddled over his word processor, typing the same line over and over: "God protect me from myself."

After an extended period of this repetitious behavior, he shifted his gaze to the video camera through which I was observing him and he shouted, "God protect me from you voyeurs! You peeping perverts! Watch, perverts, and I'll give you something to peep at!"

The deviant turned, with his rear parts facing the camera, and he lifted his smock to reveal his buttocks. He then spread his buttocks and passed gas in a very noisy way. "Here's to you, perverts!" he shouted as he engaged in this behavior. Finally, he laughed and his own humor stimulated him to the point where he could hardly contain himself. He was holding his own sides while he laughed, as if he were trying to keep himself from bursting.

Back at his word processor, he stared at the machine and said, "Ah, what's the use? Wiping me out. That's what they're doing…bit by bit. Pit by pit. Shit by shit." Staring at the sheet of paper, he shook his head, then grabbed the paper, crumpled it into a ball, and threw it over his shoulder to join the other debris on his floor.

Sitting very still, he froze into an erect position, stared an unblinking stare, began to breathe rapidly, and then clasped his hands against his temples, shuddered, became pale, and grunted, "Ugh!" Then, in response to the migraine, he vomited onto the floor near his word processor. His breathing slowed down. His eyes developed a hazy, limp-lidded look. He clenched his teeth and held the top of his head with his hands, squinted his eyes, and moaned. Then he shook his head several times as tears rolled down his cheeks.

Getting up with a sigh, he shuffled slowly to the scoop-back chair, moaning in pain as he moved along. He slumped into the chair and stared blankly at the black velvet wall, breathing slowly. Then he shouted at the wall, "What's hiding behind those eyes? Why are you snarling?" He put his left arm in front of his face in self-defense and leaped up so that he was now standing on the chair.

"Cats!" he screamed. "I see the three of you coming at me!" He was climbing the backrest of his chair now, trying to get away from the cats. "Get them out of here! They'll chew me up!" he shouted, pushing against the apparition.

He began acting as if an animal had a grip on his left leg. "No!" he shouted. "Get away!" Then he looked around him and said, "Gone. They're gone now, damn them."

Just as he was beginning to relax in his chair he let his right arm hang down. Pulling it back suddenly, he shouted toward the floor, "Snakes! Hundreds of them! Get them away from me!"

Overwhelmed by the hallucination, he stared at the camera and screamed for help. "Get them out of here, will you? Can't you see them?" He shook his head. "Gone now. They're gone. Where are they from? Where did they go? Who's to say? Who's to know?"

Soon he went to the dart board and when he threw the three darts at the board he came close to the bull's-eye each time. But close was not enough for him. He became angry and made an obscene gesture at the board.

Next, he went to the lowest shelf of his bookcase and took a book titled *Faust: Part One*. "There was a king once reigning, Who had a big black flea, And loved him past explaining, As his own son were he. He called his man of stitches; The tailor came straightaway; Here, measure the lad for breeches, and measure his coat, I say!"

The deviant stopped reading and burst out laughing. "Where oh where has my little flea gone? Where oh where can she be?" He looked around. "Where can you be, you sucking flea?" He looked under his arm. "Are you sucking me?" He lifted his smock and examined his pubic hair. "Are you draining me? Where are you, flea? And spider? And ant? Where are you three? Hiding from me?"

He threw his *Faust* in the air and it landed on his utility table. Then he banged on his bookcase several times, shouting, "Come out to play, you creeps!" The ant scurried out of the bookcase, leaving the space where *Faust* had been located, next to a book by Freud. Then the ant made a straight line across the floor to the shower drain. Kneeling over the drain and peering down, Doctor Fayne asked, "What are you hiding from, ant? Yourself? Don't you know that wherever you go, there you are? Do you prefer your dark, slimy pit to the open air? Ah, who cares? The time is out of joint, but so what? This joint is also out of time."

RESEARCH NOTE:
Our research indicates that the quotation, "The time is out of joint" is from a partially acceptable author named William Shakespeare. The specific work cited is Hamlet I.

Back in his chair, the deviant made some angry statements with his eyes closed. "No hope? Doomed for eternity? Lost forever? So what? Get lost!" He shook his head and then hit his head with his fist several times. "Get out of my head, damn you!"

When he calmed down, he rose and took his food tray from the dumb-waiter, inserted it into the microwave oven, cursed the oven for being so slow, and then sat down to eat his carrots-and-peas, mashed potato, chopped beef, and mixed vegetable soup. After taking one sip of the soup, he leaped up, spat the soup onto the floor, looked at the camera, waved his fist, and then he spat into the soup several times. Finally, holding the soup bowl toward the camera he yelled, "Try it, you'll like it!" But he did not throw it. Instead, he paused and declaimed, "When in doubt, eat, drink and be merry. For tomorrow we die!"

Back in his chair, he ate small portions of his meal and then said, "Jack Sprat could eat no fat, his wife could eat no lean, and so between the two of them they licked the platter clean. Oh, yes. Something else, too. Pussy Cat ate the dumplings! Mamma stood by and cried, Oh, fie! Why did you eat the dumplings? Ah, yes. Oh, my. What I'd give for some no-fat, no-lean dumplings. Oh me. Oh, my. What I'd give for..."

The usual click, buzz, and hum signaled the opening of the electrified steel door. Sniffing as he entered, Sumner said, "I see you've got a lot for me to clean up, Fayne."

Doctor Fayne looked at Sumner. "Breathes there a man with soul so dead who never to himself has said, My kingdom for a sniff...or maybe a snuff."

"You're pretty messed up today, huh Fayne? You're sort of pathological, I think. Maybe they'll give you a little trip to The Trap, Fayne. Or put you in a patho shelter and straighten out your head a little with some Cranial Reorganization Therapy. Yeah, the CRT will straighten you out."

Sumner started his portable vacuum cleaner, began cleaning, and then motioned for the deviant to move so that he could clean his area. The Doctor would not move. Sumner waved his hand in an animated way. The effect was instantaneous. Doctor Fayne shuddered, had massive tremors and contortions, and when he had composed himself he accepted Sumner's suggestion and moved.

When the vacuuming was done, Sumner ordered Doctor Fayne to the center of the floor, left the triangle, activated the overhead hoses, and thoroughly cleaned the triangle and its occupant.

When Sumner came into the triangle again and put the remaining compacted debris into the waste bin, he said, "The Kuh...Kuh...Keeper wants to see you, Fayne. So let's get going."

Doctor Fayne went to the black velvet wall, looked at it as if it were a mirror, and said, "Hold up a sec, Slumner. I have to fix my tie."

"You haven't got a tie on, Fayne." His attendant waved his hand again to communicate with the deviant's implanted device which was activated by a motion detector.

"Ouch! Enough! I'm coming, Slumner. See! Look! I come! Ugh!" He beat his breast like an aborigine. "Ugh! Slumner say come! Doctor Fayne comes!"

As they walked along the corridor to the Clean Room, Doctor Fayne heard a voice. "Brother Victor? Why, of course I recognized your voice. Yes, I have it memorized, word for word. How could I forget Richard Cory by Robinson. I'll recite it for you now. No, I certainly don't want the whip. I'll recite it the right way."

Sumner asked, "Are you hearing things again, Fayne?"

Doctor Fayne put his finger to his lips and said softly to Sumner, "Shh. It's Brother Victor. I have to recite my poem for him...now. You know how strict he is."

The deviant's voice began to fade as he recited quietly. Then he raised his voice so I could hear him. "'And admirably schooled in every grace: In fine, we thought that he was everything...So on we worked, and waited for the light, And went without the meat, and cursed the bread; And

Richard Cory, one calm summers night, Went home and put a bullet through his head.'"

The Doctor flinched as if he had received a heavy blow. "God, that hurts! Why do you whip me, Brother Victor? I memorized it word for word. Besides, we never even had that poem as an assignment. I did it as a writing exercise for extra credit."

He leaped to the other side of the corridor. "What did I do wrong? Please tell me. Oh, you say I should not have left out the apostrophe when I wrote the words 'summers night'? You're punishing me because of one apostrophe?"

After listening for a response, he said, "It's either all right or all wrong? There's no in between? But I don't think that's...No! Not again, Brother Victor! All right. I'll try harder next time. I'll..." He put his hand to his ear. "Are you still there? You're gone?"

Doctor Fayne said to Sumner, "He comes. He goes. Where from? Where to? Who knows?" Looking at the camera, he asked, "Do they know?"

Sumner replied, "They're watching every move you make, Fayne. And they're listening. They're going to help you become very healthy. Remember the motto: WE ARE CONCERNED."

The crease in Doctor Fayne's forehead deepened. "Concerned? Burned? Interned? Interred? The Trap? Is that where we're headed? To The Trap?"

"You're going to see The Kuh...Kuh...Keeper, Fayne, like I told you. So keep your nose clean and watch your mouth and stop acting up and maybe you won't get thrown into The Trap. Maybe I won't be sweeping up your ashes."

Hearing a rumbling noise in the distance, the Doctor said, "Is that noise coming from The Trap?"

"No, I think it's one of the FRN bombs going off," said Sumner. "They'll get caught though. Just like they'll catch that writer Lance Crowne. Pretty soon the FRN trouble makers and Crowne will be in a patho shelter and that will be the end of them and their FRN terror."

"FRN? Or do you mean FUN? One letter can make the difference, right?"

"Don't you know the Federation of Rising Nations is the FRN, Fayne? They blame the AEC for all their problems. But we aren't to blame."

"AEC? Or do you mean HEC? What the heck's the difference, huh? One letter, that's the difference."

"It's AEC, Fayne. Alliance of Enterprising Countries. The FRN's the enemy. The news was saying last night they're claiming responsibility for planting bombs around our big cities. But we'll have them under control soon. Chairman Cashin said so last night in a special telecast from Philiston."

"Cashin? That's smashin'!" Doctor Fayne laughed. "Is he dashin'? Or crashin'?"

"You're way over the border, Fayne. No use talking to you, I guess."

Doctor Fayne became silent and remained that way during the washing procedure in The Clean Room. He did not utter another word until they reached the short corridor leading to The Keeper's chamber.

Then he stopped and refused to go into the chamber. "Not a chance!" he shouted. "I'm not going in there and..." After a slight movement of Sumner's hand and some motivational energy, Doctor Fayne changed his mind and shuffled along the corridor toward The Keeper's chamber.

"Come right ahead toward my golden door, Doctor Fayne," said The Keeper's amplified voice. "I have been waiting for you." The Keeper instructed Sumner to leave. "Come right ahead, Doctor. Come into my chamber."

The Doctor muttered, "This is where he throws me in his Trap and makes chopped beef out of me. Charcoal broiled." Shuddering, he stepped through the entrance, got the automated tranquilizer and memory stimulator doses, and warily stopped.

From the blurry golden circle on the screen-like wall, The Keeper's voice calmly urged the Doctor to come to the edge of the oval gold velvet rug. But the Doctor balked. It was necessary for him to be motivated with high amplification of his own rebellious words. When the reverberations stopped there were tears pouring down the Doctor's cheeks.

"We need your cooperation," said The Keeper. "Time is of the essence."

"Take your time and tuck it," replied Doctor Fayne.

"I see you are resisting the tranquilizers today," said The Keeper as a jolt of motivational electricity coursed up the Doctor's legs and sent his body into spasms. The shock left him with minor tremors and a look of horror on his face.

"I invite you now to come to the edge of the oval gold velvet rug in a spirit of cooperation. It is in your best interest to cooperate."

"Cooperate. Yes, cooperate." As the Doctor was guided onto the rug, his fear seemed to be lessening and his eyes took on a glazed look. Then he assumed his position on the first step, with his chin resting on his forearms which were folded on the armrest rail of the kneeling apparatus.

"We have much to discuss today, Doctor Fayne. In our last session you were explaining your disillusionment with the changes in society. Acting as a reactionary during the Period of Radical Change, you found yourself being paradoxically viewed as a radical. You were losing friends, becoming isolated, and your marriage was beginning to become less intimate. As we closed our last session, you were saying that you were losing confidence."

"Yes, I was losing confidence."

"Perhaps your neuro-hypersensitivity was a problem for you. Our sensitivity tests indicate that you are in the 95th percentile when it comes to reacting to stimuli."

The Doctor said nothing.

"Tell me about your relationship with Anna."

The Doctor stared at the blurry circular area on the screen-like wall. "She began to question me about all kinds of things. How I spent my time. What my goals were. Why I thought the way I did. Then she took whatever I told her and used it against me. She changed from an agreeable person to a disagreeable one. When I began protesting openly against the Period of Radical Change in my *Journal*, she became more and more critical. But I told her I had to do what I had to do. It was a matter of principle."

"How did she respond?"

"By becoming more argumentative, contentious, and vulgar. She told me I could shove my principles up my rectum. Also, she began to withdraw sexually. Instead of sharing some time with each other in my bed or hers, she just retreated to her own room and her own bed. At the same time, she was becoming very interested in women's rights. She saw men as the enemy and began to lump me in with the whole male world. So, in her eyes I became the enemy, too."

"What was your reaction to her behavior?"

"I felt powerless over her behavior, so I shifted my energy and concentrated on my studies, my classroom work, my *Journal*."

"Did you still have sexual intercourse with her?"

"Very seldom. And then it was always on her terms. It wasn't the mutual chemistry that we had in the beginning. By this time the women's movement had advanced from feminism to narcissism. She was self-centered to the maximum. So eventually I decided to be celibate rather than experience her domineering approach to sex. We lived separate lives under the same roof."

"What about alcohol consumption?"

"We both still drank, but not together anymore. I sipped my bourbon for relaxation."

"Daily?"

"Not necessarily."

"You do not feel you were dependent on it at that time?"

"Well, there were times when I would drink too much. But that would be followed by a period of moderation. I've never enjoyed being out of control."

"You consider yourself a moderate person?"

"Most of the time. Yet I've always had a tendency to give excessive energy to projects that interested me. So, there were times when my priorities conflicted with Anna's. We were both highly work-oriented, but in her case, even though she began to think of me as an enemy, she was like a saint when it came to the unfortunate people she counseled.

"She would always go the extra mile. I did my work well, too, but there was something special about Anna. She would do anything for anybody without complaining, even if they came to her for help in the evening when she was already exhausted. I knew it was taking a lot out of her, but she wouldn't have it any other way.

"She was much more than a psychotherapist and a social worker. She helped whores who were down on their luck with the same care she gave to upscale clients. She visited people who were on the verge of starvation and helped get them assistance. She consoled the elderly and counseled the young. She was the embodiment of love and compassion.

"But there was a definite shift in her attitudes and a new intensity emerged. It overshadowed the tender love and affection and companionship we had experienced before. There was a real split between her feelings for me and her outgoing love to others. There was a...there was...a...real... split...there was a...real..."

"Stay with me, Doctor Fayne. We are making good progress. Don't drift away now into inane babbling. There is some clarification required and I need your cooperation."

"Yes, cooperation."

"I want to clarify the time element. You have mentioned

your resistance to changes in society, and the changes in Anna's attitudes. Pinpoint when this was happening."

"Pinpoint. Pinhead. Counterpoint. Counterfeit. Attitudes. Platitudes..."

"Cease that inane word play, please."

"Inane. Insane. Element. Excrement. Clarify. Petrify..."

"I cannot abide the nonsensical rhyming. It is such a waste of important time. You will need to return to your triangle now, Doctor Fayne. You will rejoin Sumner and return to your triangle...and rest."

"Yes...rest. Rest in peace."

Case Report Disposition
Observation to be continued.

5

Case Report
Deviant: Fayne, Wylie, Ph.D.
Number: 1
Shelter: Bentham Deviant Shelter
Province: Avernus
Housing: Total Scrutiny
Therapy: Time Void
Technique: Observation and Dialogue
Condition: To be ascertained.

<u>Summary of Session Number 5</u>

The deviant was in a monkish, bookish mode when I next observed him. He had been reading and was taking his book to the bookcase, where he put it back in the top shelf. When he turned to go to his chair, he muttered, "Is that you, Skuld?"

He put his thumb and index finger behind his ear, pressed them together at the point where his ear was joined to his scalp, and removed the flea. Then he held his hand a short distance from his eyes and asked, "Where have you been, Skuld? What have you been doing? Leaping frantically into the future? Anxiously heaving yourself around, looking for answers to questions without answers?

"I believe your basic problem is that you lack faith, Skuld. If you had more faith, you would be more content and you would not always feel the need to leap, leap, leap. You could learn something from Urda instead of considering her a throwback to ancient times. I think you feel superior to her because you have gone through a complete metamorphosis, but I think you overemphasize the desirability of change.

"Consider Urda's integrity throughout her lifespan, while she casually ambles around on her four pairs of legs and waits for prey to come to her. She weaves her webs with her spinnarets, sits back, and survives very nicely while you leap around from one creature to another, flying through the air without obvious wings, looking for new sources of your life-sustaining fluid, never satisfied, never resting, always searching. But that is your nature, I suppose, and why should I presume to alter it?

"Go, Skuld." He opened his thumb and index finger, and the flea leaped off toward the nearest corner of the triangle. "Keep leaping, if you must, until you wear yourself out."

He sat in the scoop-back chair once again, and began staring at the black velvet wall. A moment later he cocked his ear and said, "Who? Dean Fylche? You say I did a wonderful job for you at the university? Well, thank you very much, but I deserve no praise. A job well done is praise enough for me. I need no other commendation.

"You say I influenced millions of people through my *Journal*? I think you may be exaggerating my capabilities, but I appreciate your kind words nevertheless. You say you are Dean Fylche but I don't seem to recall your name. When and where did I work with you? No answer. Are you still there? She must have gone again, back to wherever it is that she came from."

He looked passively at the black velvet wall, heaved a sigh, and said softly, "I am thankful to God for all He has given me. I am content to serve Him here in my hermitage."

Suddenly his dark brown eyes widened and he said, "You present a very beautiful picture with your white dress, young lady. You look like a saint. Your name is Anna? That is a very nice name. I believe it derives from the Hebrew, meaning grace. No. I do not recall making your acquaintance.

"You call me Doctor Wylie Fayne? The name is not mine. I am simply Brother Wylie in The Order of The Holy Chalice and I have no desire for more of an identity. If you need a salutation, please feel free to just call me Brother.

"You say you always had great respect for me? I have no idea what I did to deserve such respect, but I would be an ingrate if I failed to accept your kind comments graciously. Even though I have no memory of ever meeting you I am pleased that you have decided to visit with me.

"You have the radiance of a painting by Raphael, my child. You seem to bring the light of God into my humble hermitage. Am I sure I have no memory of you? Quite sure, my child. Quite...oh, you have gone.

"Your visit is ended. But I am content. I have my contemplation on which to reflect, and I have my lectures to deliver to the viewing audience. I am content to dedicate myself to the monastic life except for the brief interludes of communication between me and the outside world via the electronic medium. I am quite content."

He rose from his chair and went over to the dumbwaiter, took the frozen food tray, put it into the automated microwave oven, and while he waited for the food to heat and the tray to glide out of the slot ready to eat, he muttered, "God will provide for us. We can be grateful for that."

Moments later the tray came out, with the meal hot but the tray itself at touchable temperature. He brought it near his utility table, which was located about as far as the chain would reach. Then he sat on the stool and crossed himself, said grace, and began slowly to eat the meal which consisted of peas, sliced carrots, mashed potatoes, and a cup of lukewarm tea.

He ate precisely half of each portion and then he brought the tray back to the dumbwaiter, nodding his head and whispering, "It is wise to avoid gluttony. A partially filled stomach will suffice."

Going to the washbowl, he washed his hands and face repeatedly and muttered, "The abundance of The Lord surrounds us." Then he went to the blow-drier, activated it, dried his hands and face, went to his bookcase, took his prayer book, and again returned to the scoop-back chair with the book in his hands.

For a while he stared straight ahead at the black velvet wall, and then he said softly, "What beautiful stars. All blue and white on that dark background. The wonders of God's universe are ours if we would only open our eyes to see them. Thank you, Lord, for all of your gifts."

He nodded his head and said, "Now, let me see." He turned the pages of the prayer book. "Here it is: O Almighty and eternal God, Whose majesty filled heaven and earth, I firmly believe that Thou art here present; that Thine all-seeing eye is upon me; that Thou knowest all things, and art most intimately present in the very center of my soul. I desire to..."

There was a click and a buzz and a hum as the electrified steel door to his triangle slid open and Sumner entered with his portable battery operated vacuum cleaner. He stood inside the triangle, jutted his face forward, and his parrot nose sniffed. Then he shook his head. "The nut case is having another clean fit."

Showing no emotion, Doctor Fayne said, "Why, it is Brother Summoner. Welcome to my hermitage, Brother. I will be with you in a moment. I am at prayer, you see." He turned his attention to the prayer book, muttered as he read, and nodded his head a few times as he agreed with the text.

Sumner came over to him and said, "The Kuh...Kuh... Keeper wants to see you, Fayne, so get up and get moving."

Doctor Fayne looked up at Sumner's broad, sallow face with its jutting chin, drooping right eyelid, and parrot nose. He said softly in a stage whisper, "Brother Summoner calls Father Abbot by another title and he gives me a name that has no familiarity, but I believe he means no harm."

He closed the prayer book, rose, and shuffled to the low book case. As he placed the book on the top shelf, he turned to Sumner and said, "I am ready to see Father Abbot now."

"Father Abbot? Listen, fella. It's The Kuh...Kuh...Keeper that wants to see you, and if you know what's good for you, you won't call him Father Abbot." He motioned the deviant toward the corridor and the steel door slid closed after them.

Doctor Fayne whispered, "Brother Summoner seems confused about Father Abbot's title. He's probably overtired from performing his duties. With God's help his memory will soon serve him better."

As they began walking along the dull silver-gray corridor with its newly installed concrete floors, there were some mild rumblings from the distance.

Sumner said, "They say there's some FRN idiots causing trouble in New Grafton, over at the airport. They're taking hostages and throwing bombs but Philiston's sending in some UEP troops, and that'll stop it. If there's anything left of them I'll probably be washing them up in The Clean Room in a couple of days to get them ready to ship off to the war."

The deviant had a placid look on his face and a slightly glazed look in his eyes as he walked along. He made no comment as Sumner told him about the latest violence in The Province.

Just a few moments later he said to Sumner, "God will provide for us, Brother Summoner. We must never forget that it is of the utmost importance for us to maintain our faith in The Lord. Faith is the opening of an inward eye, you see. The eye of the heart. We must view The Lord with the eyes of our hearts. We must......"

Sumner grunted. "I never saw such a screwed-up nut case as you, do you know that? You better not give The Kuh...Kuh...Keeper any of that religious stuff when you talk to him or you're going to end up in The Trap. Did you hear what I said, Fayne, about The Trap?"

The deviant said nothing at first but when Sumner repeated his question, he replied, "It is all a matter of viewpoint, Brother Summoner. One man's trap is another man's paradise. There are those who would be totally thwarted if they were to exchange their position for mine, but I am quite content with my solitude, you see. I am satisfied to remain silent and read and write and meditate and lecture, so there is nothing about my status that even remotely resembles the concept you call The Trap. With the good Lord there are no traps, Brother Summoner. The Lord provides for His own, and..."

Sumner interrupted him. "You don't make any sense, Fayne. I don't know which is worse, the clean fits and your lectures or the times when you're a rotten slob and speak nothing but bunk."

The Doctor said nothing as he moved slowly through the dimly lit corridor, with Sumner following behind him, vacuum cleaner in hand. Before they reached The Clean Room, Sumner muttered a few more things about the deviant's extreme behavior, yet the deviant remained silent.

At The Clean Room, the deviant followed Sumner's instructions without hesitation. He removed his smock and slippers, got into the wash basket, extended his arm for the shot from Sumner's medication gun, held his breath and closed his eyes during the wash and rinse cycles, then dressed himself in the clean smock and slippers when the washing and drying process was completed.

"The fresh robe gives one a feeling of relief and renewal," he said as they left The Clean Room.

"Relieve your ass on your fresh robe," muttered Sumner irritably as the door slid shut behind them.

"I would never defecate on my fresh robe, Brother Summoner. As you know, cleanliness is next to Godliness, and the outer condition tends to reflect the inner. We should strive for hygiene without and within, Brother Summoner."

"Hygiene your ass," responded Sumner. "Get moving, Fayne, and knock off the diversions. You know The Kuh...Kuh...Keeper's waiting, and if we keep him waiting too long, it'll be The Trap for both of us."

"Traps are a matter of perspective," said Doctor Fayne. "It all depends on how you look at your circumstances. As for me, I..."

"Why don't you just be quiet and say your prayers?" suggested Sumner.

"Yes, it is good to say prayers, and we can never say too many of them. Even as we walk to chapel for vespers...or is it compline, Brother Summoner...we should use the time at our disposal to silently offer up to The Lord the very steps we are taking as we move along. Is it vespers we are going to...or is it time for compline, Brother?"

"I don't know what this vespers and compline bunk is that you're talking about, Fayne, and as for the time, since you are getting Time Void Therapy here, you don't have to worry about the time. If it's day or night, it's all the same for you."

The deviant nodded. "I am sure it is all the same in the eyes of The Lord, too, Brother Summoner. For what is time but a mental construct devised by man to serve his own ends? I need no reference to time, Brother. I am quite content to function on the eternal plane."

"Well, get your contented eternal plane body moving then, Fayne. We don't have time to listen to all that bunk, and The Kuh...Kuh...Keeper isn't much for waiting for guys that sling the bull. Just because you're getting Time Void Therapy doesn't mean we've got all day."

Doctor Fayne said nothing, and soon they reached the point where Sumner told him to go to the right along the short corridor leading to The Keeper's chamber. The amplified message from The Keeper told Sumner to leave, then ordered, "Come right ahead, Doctor Fayne, toward my golden door."

The deviant whispered, "He thinks I am someone else. He gives me the title of Doctor, which has never been bestowed on me." He walked up to The Keeper's golden door, which was closed. Then he paused. His eyes opened wide as he nodded his head and smiled at the door. He said, "Why, thank you, your Eminence. But I deserve no special honor. I have simply been doing my duty. Yes, I understand. Well, if you feel the honor is merited, I will naturally accept your decision with all due respect and humility. Yes, your Eminence, I will...."

The Keeper's voice boomed out. "Come toward my golden door, Doctor Fayne"

The door clicked, buzzed, hummed, and slid open. The Doctor shook his head as the vision of the Cardinal faded. Then he moved forward slowly as the tranquilizer and memory stimulator injections did their job.

The door slid shut behind him, and Doctor Fayne threw himself on his knees on the bare metallic floor and crossed himself, saying loudly, "In the name of the Father, and of the Son, and of the Holy Ghost. Amen."

Then he recited, "'And the people went forth, and brought. And they made themselves tabernacles every man on the top of his house, and in their courts, and in the street, of the water gate, and in the street of the gate of Ephraim. And all the assembly of them that were returned from the captivity, made tabernacles, and dwelt in tabernacles; for since the days of Josue the son of Nun the children of Israel had not done so, until that day; and there was exceeding great joy.'"

"Enough!" exclaimed The Keeper. "Get up, Doctor. Time is of the essence. Take off your slippers and come to my steps."

"Yes, Father Abbot." Doctor Fayne nodded, rose, took off his slippers, left them at the edge of the golden oval rug, and stepped on the rug. He nodded his head a few times, and muttered, "Lead us not into temptation." Continuing to nod his head, he crossed the rest of the rug.

"Kneel on the first step," ordered The Keeper.

"Yes, Father Abbot."

"I am not your Father Abbot," said The Keeper. "I am your Keeper and I am concerned about you. I want to help you become normal, Doctor Fayne. For the good of the economy, I want to assist you in reaching your full potential as a member of society."

The deviant whispered to himself, "Father Abbot must be tired. He is saying things that do not relate to our life here at the monastery. But with a good night's sleep he will undoubtedly be himself tomorrow."

"Do not whisper to yourself when I address you," ordered The Keeper.

"As you wish, Father Abbot."

"Do not call me Father Abbot."

"As you wish."

There was no dialogue for a few moments. Then Doctor Fayne's eyes began to develop a heavily glazed look. His eyelids began to droop almost to a shut position. His head sunk down so that his chin was resting on his folded arms as he kneeled there staring at the blurry golden circle in the center of the gold screen-like wall.

"I believe you are reaching the appropriate condition for our dialogue, Doctor. Tell me your name."

"Wylie Fayne."

"Tell me your occupation."

"Educator."

"Tell me the highest rank you have held in the field of education."

"Professor of Philosophy and Department Chair."

"Now, Doctor, let us proceed with The Unveiling. During our last session you were telling me that you were practicing celibacy to avoid Anna's domineering approach to sexual intimacy."

"Yes, that was the way it was for a while. And then a kind of seduction began. As I was growing more humble and less professorial and more Christian in a down-to-earth way, Anna was growing less like a radical feminist and very methodically making herself more alluring. She was changing her appearance to tempt me and invited me to her room late at night. She would greet me with nothing on except her sheer lingerie. But I hadn't forgotten the pain of her previous scorn and abuse, so I maintained my celibacy."

"What happened next, Doctor? Please continue. But first I have a reward for you. After reviewing my record of our last meeting, it became obvious to me that we are now making excellent progress and it would be appropriate for you to move upward to the second step."

There was a buzz and click and hum, and the armrest assembly on its tracks moved slowly upward from the first step to the second.

The deviant remained kneeling on the first step, with a bewildered look in his eyes. Then The Keeper said, "Rise now, Doctor Fayne, and move upward to the second step. You have my permission."

The Doctor nodded his head politely. Then he rose slowly, taking his new position on the second of the three steps while staring straight ahead toward the blurry circle in the middle of the golden screen.

He rested his chin on his folded arms as The Keeper instructed him. "From now on you are to proceed immediately to the second step, not to pause on the first, and not to attempt to move up to the third step without my express permission. You see, the third step will only be achieved at the completion of The Unveiling. Do you understand me, Doctor?"

"Yes, I'm sure I understand you quite well."

"Since time is of the essence, Doctor, I request that you try not to ramble today. Please answer my questions as directly as possible."

The deviant nodded toward the blurry circle. "As you say,

that's what I'll do."

There was another pause as the Doctor's eyes became more and more glazed. Then The Keeper said, "Now we will begin again. Continue where you left off, Doctor. Explain the progress of the seduction."

"Her seductive behavior worked on me and soon I was planning my own seduction. Celibacy be damned. Now my craving for her was all consuming. My plan went very well, as all my plans used to do once I set my mind to something. After a while it was a question of who was seducing whom, as Anna became more and more assertive. You might say it was a mutual seduction.

"It was spring, I remember. The forsythia were bursting out with their yellow blossoms and Anna was bursting with passion. I had rid myself of all doubts. I could relinquish celibacy or not; either outcome would be fine. There was such pleasure in our passion now. Such total love. Such affection. Such warmth. Such anticipation.

"It was right after Easter, I recall, on a warm spring night. I was in my study, going over the editorial accounts, when the fragrance came into my nostrils. The new perfume she had begun to wear was powerfully seductive. Soon she was next to me, hovering over me, touching me softly as I tried to concentrate on my work."

"Am I distracting you, dear?" she asked as she breathed on my neck. "Am I making it hard for you to concentrate?"

"No, dear. You're not making it hard, you're making it impossible. You are so irresistible."

"Do you want to resist? Do you prefer your celibacy? Do you want me to leave?" she teased me with passionate sweetness.

"No, sweetheart, I never want you to feel...I never...I never want you to...I never..."

"Pull yourself together, Doctor. You were beginning to make some progress. But now you seem to have reached a block that is keeping you from delving deeper into the truth."

"Block? Aha! It rhymes with rock! Hickory Dickory dock. The mouse ran up the..."

"Cease and desist from the inane rhyming, Doctor. Apparently, we will have to terminate our session earlier than usual. I have no tolerance today for such behavior when time is of the essence. You may put on your slippers now and return with Sumner to your triangle. Now depart," insisted The Keeper, "without delay."

"Without delay," repeated the Doctor, who finally made his way out of the chamber to join his attendant. "Without delay," he muttered as he went into the hallway. "Yes, I am departing now...without delay...to rest. Rest in peace."

Case Report Disposition
Observation to be continued.

6

Case Report
Deviant: Fayne, Wylie, Ph.D.
Number: 1
Shelter: Bentham Deviant Shelter
Province: Avernus
Housing: Total Scrutiny
Therapy: Time Void
Technique: Observation and Dialogue
Condition: To be ascertained.

Summary of Session Number 6

When I began to observe the deviant's behavior today, his triangle was in a state of perfect cleanliness and there was a peaceful look on his face. He sat at his word processor typing the line "God will provide for us." Then he paused, nodded at the words on the sheet before him, and a half-smile appeared on his bony black-and-gray bearded face.

Soon he got up from the tubular plastic stool where he had been typing and he went over to the washbowl, squirted some liquid soap onto the palms of his hands, activated the water faucet, and scrubbed his hands for several minutes while whispering, "Yes, God will provide for us."

He went to the scoop-back chair, sat fairly erect, put the palms of his hands on his knees, closed his eyes, slowed down his breathing, muttered, "The Crucifix," took in another breath, muttered "The Crucifix" again as he exhaled, and did this practice for several minutes.

Then he opened his eyes, which had a glazed look now, and he looked up at the camera to his right and said, "Yes, we may begin." A half smile appeared on his face as he addressed the camera. "God will provide for us," he said. "That is our thought for today. You see, it is very important that we have faith in The Lord at all times and never question His will for us.

"Let us consider what Thomas Merton said about The Lord's ability to provide for us. Let us think about our faith." As he shuffled toward his bookcase, he addressed the video camera. "I consider myself very fortunate to have such an excellent scriptorium here in the monastery. Father Abbot has been kind enough to permit me to bring several important volumes back here to my hermitage."

Taking the book titled *New Seeds of Contemplation* by Thomas Merton, he opened the black-and-white volume to the middle, turned the pages carefully, and then said, "Here we are. Let us consider how Merton puts it. 'Faith is first of all an intellectual assent. It perfects the mind, it does not destroy it. It puts the intellect in possession of Truth which reason cannot grasp by itself.'"

He turned two more pages. "Here he says, 'Faith is the opening of an inward eye, the eye of the heart, to be filled with the presence of divine light.' Think about those words. Reflect on their beauty."

He cautioned viewers: "Please do not fail to remember our agreement that we are from God, and that He never leaves us. We must believe in Him, love Him, and have faith in Him." Getting up, he went back to the bookcase, placed the book carefully in the spot from which he had taken it, and removed another book with dark blue lettering titled *Humanistic Poetry.*

Back in his scoop-back chair he flipped the pages very carefully and then said to the camera, "Here we are reading from William Blake in a verse called The Clod and The Pebble. 'Love seeketh not itself to please, nor for itself hath any care, But for another gives its ease, And builds a heaven in hell's despair....Love seeketh only Self to please, to bind another to its delight, Joys in another's loss of ease, And builds a hell in heaven's despair.'

"So, my good people, let us build our heaven from hell's

despair, and let us love God without expecting any favors from Him. Now, after a brief pause for a message of interest to us all, we will be back with more."

The deviant then put away the poetry book and began to pace around his triangle, faster and faster. His mood shifted from peace to anger and he started to destroy the neatness that had existed before. This continued until His triangle was nearly totally filthy but not quite to the point of putrefaction that would activate the automated hoses.

He flung himself onto his typing stool and hunched over his word processor with his raunchy smock bunched up on his knees, and over and over he typed the line: "God preserve me from my enemies."

After typing it several times on the same sheet of paper, he crumpled it into a ball, spat a blob of phlegm onto the ball, and heaved it over his shoulder, not looking to see where it might land. He swung around on the stool and looked up at the cameras above, rotated his middle finger at them, and shouted, "Up your cockeyed lenses! Get your damn Cyclops eye off me, will you?"

In just a few moments he had transformed himself from a calm video lecturer to an angry deviant performing for the camera. "Okay, you peeping pervert, here's to you!" He leaped onto the stool, hitched up his smock and stood staring defiantly at the camera for a moment. Then he began waving fists and extending middle fingers at the camera, first in slow motion, then in upward thrusts.

He kept this up for several minutes. Then, when he was about to leap down again and was crouching to do so, a look of fear came over his face, his eyes widened with horror, and he shouted, "Yikes. Look at the scissors cutting off that huge pecker! And the blood dripping! Filling up the place. No!" He held his hands tightly over his ears.

"Not mine. Not now, damn you!" He cocked his ear. "I'm not the one who betrayed her. Not me. Don't cut it off. I ..."

He crouched down, holding his hands tightly over his private parts as he huddled on top of the stool. Then he shook his head and blinked his eyes and slowly placed one leg, and then the other, on the floor. Then he said to himself, "They are destroying me one part at a time."

He shuffled through garbage and spit and balls of discarded typing paper, threw himself into the scoop-back chair and began to look toward the black velvet wall. Then he said loudly, "This is the forest primeval. The forest is primarily evil. The evil is not prime. The evil is time. Prime evil. Time evil. Hah! Prime time evil." He looked up at the camera. "Where did you hide my prime time? Ah, shove it. Who needs your fouled-up, snow-jobbing sleez box?" He waved his middle finger at the television. "Up yours!"

To emphasize his last exclamation, he stamped his gray-slippered foot onto a book lying under his chair. Then he leaned forward, picked up the large red-and-yellow bound volume, wet around the edges from contact with a puddle of urine near his washbowl, and he looked at the title: *The Basic Writings of Sigmund Freud.* Then he shoved his thumb about one-third of the way into the pages.

Squinting, he read out loud, "How do these stairs and this woman get into my dream? The shame of not being fully dressed is undoubtedly of a sexual character; the servant of whom I dream is older than I. When I pay my morning visit at this house I am usually seized with a desire to clear my throat; the sputum falls on the stairs. There is no spittoon on either of the two floors, and I consider that the stairs should be kept clean not at my expense, but rather by the provision of a spittoon."

The deviant shook his head, cleared his throat, and blew the wad of spit about half way across the floor. "Hah. The stairs should be kept clean not at my expense. You said it, Sigmund. Not at my expense." He cleared his throat again and once more he went "ptooey." Laughing, he shouted,

"The sputum falls where the sputum falls."

Then he let a third wad of spit go flying, slammed the book shut, threw it in the air, and watched it land on a pile of excrement he had dumped there earlier. Laughing, he said, "Now you're on the floor with your shit, Sigmund. When I get around to id...I mean 'it'...I'll order you a spittoon. But I don't have much time for errands. In fact, I have no time at all. Hah. No time."

He slumped back and became very quiet in the scoop-back chair, stared up at the ceiling for a few moments, and then his jaw muscles rippled, his teeth clenched, his eyes almost completely closed, and his hands flew up and pressed hard against his temples.

Then he grunted, "Hrgh. Argh. Oh, shit! Jee-sus! Argh." He sat erectly in the chair, then threw his head forward, still clenching the temples with the palms of his hands as the migraine intensified. With his forehead almost touching his knees, he groaned and sighed for several minutes.

He shouted, "Damn!" Then he vomited on his own feet, sighed, and slumped back into the scoop-back chair. For a few moments he remained motionless, with his eyes closed. Then he sat bolt upright and looked around. "Whose is this voice that awakens me? Or does it aweaken me? Is it you, Death? Have you come? Was that you shouting in my ear 'Your time is here'? I heard you say it. But no. It was a softer voice. A feminine one. Time? No? Did you say crime? That was it. Your crime is here. What crime? Who would accuse me of a crime?"

He looked around the triangle. "You accuse me and then hide. Where are you?" He got down on his knees and began crawling around the floor, looking for the source of the voice. "'Your crime is here', you said. Well, I can't find you."

Cupping his right hand around his right ear, he said, "You say you're the abandoned bride? What bride? I can hear you, but I can't see you. Why can't I see you?" He looked toward the velvet wall. "I see you now, with your white dress. You say I betrayed you? I never betrayed anybody. You saw God on a crucifix? You're Anna who? I don't know any Anna."

He began rubbing his eyes hard and shaking his head rapidly. Then he started pushing his hands away from his face, as if pushing an object or a person, and he shouted, "Get out of my eyes!"

He slumped back into the chair, breathed heavily, and kept shaking his head back and forth and muttering, "No, no, no" for several minutes. Then he began to breathe more slowly, and his facial muscles seemed to relax slightly and he looked as if he might doze off. Then he sat up, reached under his thigh, took his thumb and index finger and held them before his eyes and shouted, "You sucking flea! Why are you sucking me? For sucking my thigh...you shall cry."

Carefully taking the flea from between the skin of his thumb and index finger, he manipulated the insect into a position between the nails of his finger and thumb. Then, with his brow creased and his teeth clenched, he rubbed the nails back and forth and pressed them together against the flea's body until the flea was motionless.

Then he shouted, "That's what you get, you blood-sucker!" He flicked the flea into a puddle of water nearby. "Suck some water for a change!"

He got up and went toward his dart board, located just to the left of center on the black velvet wall. Taking the three darts from the spot where they were adhering to the bull's-eye, he walked backward slowly to a spot near his utility table, and took aim. One by one the three darts flew through the air. The first landed above the bull's-eye. The second stuck to the friction-inducing surface just below the bull's-eye. The third, after he carefully gauged the distance and made corrections for previous errors, landed right in the middle of the black bull's-eye.

He stood with hands on hips, looking at the darts. Then he

nodded his head and said, "Not bad." Shaking his head, he muttered, "Ah, what's the use? Who cares? My life is not my own. I've cooked my own goose. But I couldn't care less."

Going to his bunk, he threw himself on it, flat on his back, and he closed his eyes. "They're killing me in bits and pieces. So what's the difference anyhow? Shove it!"

He lay there for a few moments and then he started muttering, "Dickory, dickory, dare, the pig flew up in the air; The man in brown soon brought him down, dickory, dickory, dare." He nodded his head, with his eyes still closed. "Ah, what the hell is the use? Dickory dare. Pigs in the air. Men in brown. Bringing me down. To hell with the whole thing."

He sat up on the bunk, threw his legs over the side, blinked his eyes a few times, rubbed his eyes with his hands and said, "Who's that in the black outfit? The dark angel? I don't know any dark angel." He nodded his head several times. Then he shook his head animatedly. "You ask who am I to question your right to sell your body? I know nothing about your rights or your body. Lock you up? I never locked anybody up. Look, I don't even know you, so will you knock off the screaming. God, what a shrill voice."

He held his hands over his ears, grimaced as if in pain, squinting as his eyes aimed at the black velvet wall. Finally, he leaped to his feet and slapped his ears hard with the palms of his hands as he yelled, "Look, I don't even know you, you nagging bitch, will you get the...ah, there, it's stopped. The bitch is gone."

Sitting on the edge of his bunk again, his head flopped down so that his chin just about touched his chest. Then he lifted his smock, examined his navel, and shouted,"Ah-hah. There we are." He pulled a small wad of lint from his navel, put it in the palm of his left hand, looked at it for several seconds, and whispered, "Yup, that's it."

Then he took the little finger of his right hand, inserted it into his right ear and took the resulting smear of ear wax, applied it to the ball of lint in his left palm, rolled the cotton into a ball between his palms and muttered, "Roll a ball...though it's small...push that ball...through the hole in the wall. Roll a ball...down the hall...show that ball...to old King Saul. Roll a ball...up the wall...and soak that ball...in vitriol. Roll a ball...and then recall that tigers crawl...before they maul. Roll a ball..."

He inserted his index finger into his right nostril, muttering, "Roll a ball...touch a ball...shove it all...up your..." He leaped up, ran toward the door, stopped a short distance from it, looked at the camera nearby, and took the ball of wax and excretion between his thumb and index finger. "Eat it! But let me cook it for you first, you ball busters!" He flung the ball against the electrified door, where it stuck and then burned to a crisp.

"I think I overcooked it. Oh my. Why oh why did I overcook it? I think I..."

First came the loud hiss, then the cleaning shower heads sprayed their pressurized, chemically treated water throughout the triangle sending the standing Doctor Fayne sprawling onto the floor and rolling him over several times as the torrents of water soaked every inch of the triangular-shaped space. After a few minutes of the washing action, all the debris had been pushed across the cement floor to the drains; what couldn't be washed down the drain stood in a soggy mass.

Then came the blasts of hot air from the ducts above, drying everything in the place, including Doctor Fayne. At the end of the sequence he sat panting on the floor near the drain, where he had also been pushed by the pressurized water. He muttered, "Up their..."

He was pulling himself to his feet by leaning on the edge of his toilet when he heard a click and a buzz. Then the electrified door slid open and in came Sumner, who saw the soggy pile of debris, leaned over, sniffed it with his parrot nose, and turned his sallow face toward the deviant with an irritated glint in his vacant blue eyes.

"How come there isn't any cleaning for me to do here, Fayne? I got a job to do, you know."

"You need a job, Slumner? A cleaning job? I'd help you out, but they just shipped my body up the creek with no paddle, and no canoe, for that matter. What brings you here? A stranger appears on my empty horizon, with weapons brandished at the ready, a parrot's face with unmatched eyes on, and a heavy fist that's all too steady.

"Welcome to my rotten triangle, stranger. It's a strange triangle, and you're a strange stranger, and I'm even stranger than you and the triangle. Strange, isn't it? What a small world it is, I mean. That is, if you see it only in the shape of a bizarre triangle." He went to his bunk and sat on the edge of it and heaved a sigh.

Sumner said, "You make no sense, Fayne." Then he went to the soggy pile in the drain area, took the Freud book, replaced it in the lower shelf of the bookcase, picked up the rest of the debris and threw it in the waste bin, and with his large nose twitching as he talked, he muttered, "Hardly anything to clean up here."

Doctor Fayne leaped onto the cot and shuddered as he stared at the floor. "He was after my foot! Look!"

Sumner looked toward where the deviant was aiming his eyes. "You're seeing things again, Fayne, like always. You're as loony as they come."

"It's bigger than a python," yelled Doctor Fayne, huddling against the wall while standing on his bunk, shaking all over.

"Listen, fella," said Sumner, coming over to him and moving his hand slowly before the Doctor's eyes. "There are no snakes, and you're coming with me to see The Kuh...Kuh...Keeper, and the Kuh...Kuh...Keeper don't like waiting around for people who see things that aren't even there, so get your body off that bunk and get moving."

Sumner lifted his hand as if to wave it.

Doctor Fayne shouted, "Don't do it!" Then he leaped off the bunk and headed for the door with Sumner following close behind. Shuffling along the silver-gray corridor with its dim lights and intermittent cameras, the Doctor began crying and screaming, "They're going to kill me now." Over and over he said it, sobbing as he shuffled along. After about the twentieth time, he suddenly stopped as a look of horror spread over his face. "The black pit is..."

"Get moving," ordered Sumner.

The deviant ignored him and jumped to the right, against the wall, and stood shuddering as he looked down toward the floor. "There's no end to it..."

"You better get moving," ordered Sumner.

The Doctor threw himself on the floor, curled up in a ball, and shouted, "The pit. The black pit. The bottomless black pit." The deviant leaped to his feet, started to go forward, then yelled, "I'm falling in the pit. ..."

Sumner told him he would bring on his own pain if he didn't comply with orders. Then Sumner said, "It's up to you, Fayne. Just keep causing your own pain by making trouble, and The Kuh...Kuh... Keeper's going to heave your body into The Trap."

"The Trap. They'll wrap me in crap and slap me in The Trap. Rap, rap, rap. Tap, tap, tap. Crap, crap, crap."

"You're really over the border now, Fayne," said Sumner. "There's no use talking to you. If I told you they caught those bomb-tossing FRN sympathizers you wouldn't even know what I was saying, would you? They threw them in a patho shelter. I was kind of wishing I'd get them here. But maybe they'll send some over for me to clean up. I guess Chairman Cashin hasn't figured what to do with them yet. They say he's got the Supreme Econocrat Council talking about the traitors right now. The traitors went against the UEP so they ought to wipe them out to set an example. They should ship them here and let the Kuh...Kuh...Keeper throw them in the Trap."

While Sumner talked, Doctor Fayne just kept shuffling along, with a tense expression on his face, stroking his beard over and over with his right hand and shaking his head back and forth slowly.

"Did you hear me, Fayne?" asked Sumner.

The deviant remained silent as they walked the corridor, and he was silent during the whole cleansing process in The Clean Room. His silence continued as he reluctantly walked to The Keeper's Chamber.

"Come right in," ordered The Keeper. "Sumner, you are excused. I have been waiting for you, Doctor Fayne."

The deviant went through the doorway, received the tranquilizer and memory stimulator shots from the automated hypodermics, and when he was inside he came to a halt, standing with arms folded and a defiant look on his face.

"Doctor, remove your slippers and place them near the edge of my oval rug."

Doctor Fayne broke his silence and shouted at the blurry golden circle in the center of the screen-like wall, "Eat shit!"

His words, amplified many times over, came reverberating back at him, pounded at his eardrums, and the pain was so intense that tears streamed down his cheeks. He clapped his hands on his ears, shut his eyes tightly, and groaned. Then finally the words stopped coming back at him, and he looked even more intently at the blurry golden circle.

"Remove your slippers and place them neatly at the edge of the oval rug. Then proceed to the steps, Doctor."

He took off his slippers and was about to put them on the floor when he drew his arm back as far as he could and threw the slippers at the blurry golden circle and shouted, "Screw!"

This time he received double the pain. The word "screw" rebounded back at his eardrums and at the same time the slippers came flying and thrashed him, knocking him to the floor. When the ear-piercing sound stopped, The Keeper ordered him to proceed to the steps without further action.

As he began to cross the rug, he felt its sensual attraction and threw himself down onto the rug and began to sigh and roll back and forth. But this was stopped by a jolt of electricity that coursed through his whole body. Finally, he went to the first step but he balked when told to go to the second step. A jolt of electricity helped him to do as The Keeper suggested.

Then The Keeper said, "Remain kneeling until the medication does its work."

A while later, when the glazed heavy-lidded look set into his eyes, he struck his breast. "I'll never tempt her or let her tempt me again." He struck his breast for the third time. "This is my solemn promise, Lord, and although I've broken my promises to you before, I ask you to help me keep these pledges, no matter what pain and suffering they may bring. Help me, God! Show me the way!"

The Keeper said, "Enough, Doctor Fayne. Quite enough of your useless praying. Now tell me more about Anna. She was engaged in a mutual seduction with you?"

"Anna. Oh Anna. Yes, she was seductive but also holding something back from me. She was acting much differently than ever before. There was something brewing in that active mind of hers. Something she didn't want to tell me about. Something she didn't...something she was afraid of...something...and then...and then...and then......"

"Doctor Fayne!" exclaimed The Keeper." We haven't even begun. You must get hold of yourself and stay with our dialogue. You have been progressing very well up till now. Please avoid drifting off. Continue."

"Yes, continue. I was terrified of the look in her green eyes. The frightening look. The secretive look. Yes, she was holding something back from me. Something she couldn't tell me about. Something she...and then... and then... and then on a confusing evening after dinner, Anna invited me to her room, but I told her I had to work on the accounts. She kept after me to visit, but I insisted that I had to do my work. She changed into sexy lingerie and did everything she could to lure me. But I held fast. Then the questions came, as I knew they would.

"I just told her that it was nothing personal, and yes, I did love her, but I had work that needed to be done, and I was sorry, but she would have to accept it. So she finally gave up and went to her room, expecting me to come to her bed later.

"But I stayed in my own room, locked the door, and prayed to God to help me hold fast to my pledge to return to celibacy again for the sake of my peace of mind. Our return to sexual intimacy had backfired. What had seemed like love had turned into abuse. So I had to take a stand.

"Late at night, as I lay there trying to sleep but having no success, I heard her light footsteps in the hallway. She tried my door. Then she knocked. But I remained motionless. She knocked louder, but I stayed where I was. She began to call out...and I wouldn't answer her...and then...and then..."

The Keeper said, "Stay with me, Doctor Fayne. Don't allow yourself to drift off. Continue, please."

The glazed look began to leave the deviant's dark brown eyes, and the intense look set in, the crease in his forehead deepened, and he muttered, "... and then...and then...and then..."

"Don't drift off," warned The Keeper. "We must go on with The Unveiling, Doctor. We are concerned about you, you see. And time is of the essence. We want to help you become very healthy. Continue, please. Remain calm and go on. Don't drift off again. Get back on the track."

Doctor Fayne's eyes did not have as much of a glazed look now, but they reflected an inner confusion. "Drifting? Track? Oh, you must mean my praying. Somehow my mind has wandered from the vespers...or is it compline?"

"Cease and desist from this ridiculous babbling about vespers and compline, Doctor. This is the Psychological Deviant Shelter in Bentham, not a monastery. There are no monasteries in The New Social System. We abolished them. Monasteries and churches were just a throwback to centuries of primitive ignorance. It is well that they are gone."

Doctor Fayne whispered, "Father Abbot must be very weary. He seems to be misunderstanding my comments. But I will not complain. I am content."

"Stop that whispering," ordered The Keeper. "Please continue."

"Yes, Father Abbot. And then...and then...and then... "His eyes lost the glazed look and they took on a look of fear. The crease in his forehead deepened and he said loudly, "Absolve, Domine, animas omnium fidelium defunctorum ab omni vinculo delictorum...Loose, O Lord, the souls of the faithful departed from every bond of sin."

"Doctor," instructed The Keeper. "Please avoid sinking into your Latin religious ruminations. Continue where you left off."

The deviant stood with his feet on the first step, spread his arms like a priest giving an animated sermon, and said, "Dies irae, dies illa solvet saeclum in favilla, Teste David cum Sibylla...Day of wrath, O Day of mourning, Lo, the world in ashes burning, Seer and Sibyl gave the warning. It..."

"Cease and desist from this Latin diversion, Doctor Fayne. Cease and...."

"Quantas tremor est futurus, Quando Judex est venturus, Cuncta stricte discussurus...O what fear man's bosom rendeth, When from heaven the Judge descendeth, On whose sentence all dependeth. Tuba mirum..."

"Enough." ordered The Keeper.

"Tuba mirum," muttered the deviant. "Wondrous sound. Tuba mirum. Tuba mirum. Tuba..."

"Stop," insisted The Keeper. "You are testing my patience

beyond my limits. If you persist with your resistance you will only succeed in activating the implanted behavior monitors and you will attract rapidly escalating pain."

The deviant looked quizzically at the blurry golden circle where the voice seemed to be coming from, shrugged his shoulders, and turned to step on the rug.

The Keeper's voice came at him. "You will not leave the steps until I permit you to leave the steps."

"Permit? Is it a temporary permit? Or a permanent permit? Or a..."

The Keeper said, "You had better get hold of yourself, Doctor. I will not tolerate your inane babbling."

"Babbling? Do you mean bubbling? Dribbling? Doubling? Ah, that's it! Wylie's bubbling while he's doubling. But Wylie who? While he waits. While he..."

"Enough," ordered The Keeper. "If you want to babble on, go do it in your own triangle. I have no time for babbling. Go and put on your slippers."

Doctor Fayne stepped down onto the rug and the sensual stimulation prompted him to throw himself onto the rug. But immediately he was jolted by electricity. The Keeper again ordered him to cross the rug and put on his slippers. He crossed the rug, but when he bent over he shoved his arm under his legs and waved his middle finger at The Keeper, shouting, "Why don't you just go tuck it...up your royal bucket!" Only after another intensive period of eardrum pain did he finally put his slippers on.

"Go out into the corridor now, and rejoin Sumner. I can see that our session must close now, Doctor. You are in a seriously resistant mode today. You have turned your mind away from reality. Go then. Go to your triangle...and rest."

"Yes, Father Abbot." He crossed himself. "In the name of the Father, and of the Son, and of the Holy Ghost. Amen."

He said, "Lead us not into temptation" and made the Sign of The Cross as he walked toward the exit door where he threw himself on his knees and prayed aloud, "Thank you, Lord, for all the blessings you have bestowed on me."

"Get up and prepare to leave my chamber, Doctor." insisted The Keeper.

"Yes, Father Abbot." Doctor Fayne muttered, "I don't know why he calls me Doctor. I am a simple monk. But I am content to accept what he says."

The door clicked and buzzed and hummed and slid open, and The Keeper ordered, "Go to your triangle, Doctor...and rest. You must go now. Sumner will take you back to your triangle."

"Yes, Father Abbot. I will rejoin Brother Summoner and return to my hermitage. Thank you, Father Abbot. May God bless you. And please pray for me. I am going to my hermitage to rest now. Rest in peace."

Case Report Disposition
Observation to be continued.

7

Case Report
Deviant: Fayne, Wylie, Ph.D.
Number: 1
Shelter: Bentham Deviant Shelter
Province: Avernus
Housing: Total Scrutiny
Therapy: Time Void
Technique: Observation and Dialogue
Condition: To be ascertained.

Summary of Session Number 7

During my next observation I noted that the deviant's triangle was spotlessly clean. The Doctor was in his immaculate gray smock, standing at the washbowl, washing his hands. In alternating sequence, he pressed the button that sent a drop of liquid soap down onto the palm of his hand, pressed another button that sent a timed flow of water from the automated faucet, scrubbed and rinsed his hands, flicked the water from his fingertips into the bowl, then started the process over again.

This went on for several minutes until he changed the cycle of activity by going to the hot-air blow-drier next to his shower, completely drying his hands.

Then he went to his typewriter, inserted a piece of white paper, and typed the line, "God is our constant friend." Soon he got up, looked down at the line on the paper, nodded his head, went to the scoop-back chair, sat down and sighed.

Next he whispered, "Which one of you is it?" He leaned over, peered behind the calf of his left leg, saw the red ant climbing up his leg, and said, "Oh, it is you, Verdandi. He put his finger down to the ant which scurried up into the palm of his hand. Then he laid the palm flat and the ant kept walking in circles on the palm.

"Why are you so agitated, Verdandi?" asked Doctor Fayne. "Why are you so ridden with anxiety? Have you no faith? Relax, Verdandi. Life goes on, you know, even when we are relaxing. Are you afraid that if you stop for a moment the whole world will stop?"

The ant still kept circling. "You obviously pay me no heed today, Verdandi. But as for me, I simply live and let live. Continue your scurrying, if you must. But I do think it implies a lack of faith.

"By the way, have you seen your flea friend, Skuld? I have not seen him leaping lately. And Urda? Where has that spider gone? No answer? You have no interest in my questions? You have no concern about the whereabouts of Urda and Skuld?

"You seem to have a selfish orientation today, Verdandi. Perhaps you would prefer to be alone." He took the ant and put it on the floor next to his chair, and watched the ant scurry in a straight line toward the drain in the corner where it disappeared into one of the openings in the grating.

"I see," said the Doctor. "You want to be alone; perhaps you need to meditate." He slumped down into the scoop-back chair, with his head resting against the top of the backrest as he stared passively toward the black velvet wall.

With his hands resting on his knees, he breathed deeply. His eyelids drooped slightly, his mouth fell open, and with each exhale he sighed out the words "Our Father" slowly. On and on he did this, for several minutes. Then he closed his eyes completely and sat silently for a while.

Rising, he said, "It is time," and went to his bookcase where he found *Modern Man In Search Of A Soul*. Taking the book to the scoop-back chair, he turned the chair so that he was facing the video camera on the ceiling above the entrance door.

"God is our constant friend," he said with great energy. "That is our thought for today, my good viewers. Let us consider some thoughts from that great healer Carl Gustav Jung. He was a psychoanalyst, philosopher and something of a theologian." He fingered the pages until he reached a chapter about two-thirds of the way through the book.

Nodding at the camera, he said. "Listen to Jung: Baptism endows the human being with a unique soul...the idea of baptism lifts a man out of his archaic identification with the world and changes him into a being who stands above it."

He gazed at the camera. "Think about that for a moment. Think about what our friend God has done for us, giving us a unique soul that truly sets us apart from the rest of the natural world."

With a half-smile he turned the pages until he found another passage. "Here we are. 'The archetypal image of the wise man, the savior or redeemer, lies buried and dormant in man's unconscious since the dawn of culture; it is awakened whenever the times are out of joint and a human society is committed to a serious error. When people go astray they feel the need of a guide or teacher or even of the physician.'"

He nodded his head and gave a knowing look to the camera. "So I say to you, my good viewers, if you feel you need a guide or teacher or physician, open your hearts and minds to our constant friend, God. Let him come to you in your dreams and on the streets, from the mouths of beggars and in great works of art and in your churches. Take him in. Receive him. Have faith in him. Accept him, even though you do not understand him. Is not that what we do with all of our friends? Don't we accept them unconditionally?"

He brought the book back to the bookcase, talking as he went. "Next to the text we have just considered, I see a small book that is easy to overlook yet very important. It is also written by Doctor Jung and is titled *The Undiscovered Self.*"

Flipping the book open at random, he said, "Yes, page 67 has some powerful insights that were written during the middle of the Twentieth Century. Let us consider these ideas.

I will read a few passages for your contemplation."

"'…it is this banding together and the resultant extinction of the individual personality that makes it so readily succumb to a dictator. A million zeroes joined together do not, unfortunately, add up to one. Ultimately everything depends on the quality of the individual, but the fatally shortsighted habit of our age is to think only in terms of large numbers and mass organizations, though one would think that the world had seen more than enough of what a well-disciplined mob can do in the hands of a single madman.

'Unfortunately, this realization does not seem to have penetrated very far, and our blindness in this respect is extremely dangerous. People go on blithely organizing and believing in the sovereign remedy of mass action, without the least consciousness of the fact that the most powerful organizations can be maintained only by the greatest ruthlessness of their leaders and the cheapest of slogans.'"

The deviant nodded. "I have always appreciated the clarity of Doctor Jung's thinking. But he was more than a secular thinker; he was also a God-fearing man, you see, and an astute observer of society. So was Charles Dickens."

He picked a book with a leather cover and gold on the edges of its pages and said, "Dickens used *A Tale of Two Cities* to show how a mob can turn to lunacy, destroy an innocent individual, and rob him of his liberty to be himself."

Nodding, he turned to a passage describing the widespread fear that accompanied the French Revolution. "'This universal watchfulness not only stopped him on the highway twenty times in a stage, but retarded his progress twenty times in a day….and he was, therefore, as little surprised as a man could be, to find himself awakened at the small inn to which he had been remitted until morning, in the middle of the night'"

The deviant looked at the camera and explained, "The

innocent traveler in France had lost all of his rights, all of his liberty, and had no voice in his own destiny. He could not even choose to have a good night's sleep. This was how it was during and after the French Revolution."

Turning to another page, he read, "'The new era began; the king was tried, doomed, and beheaded. The Republic of Liberty, Equality, Fraternity, or Death declared for victory or death…there was no pause, no pity, no peace, no interval of relenting rest, no measurement of time….a law of the Suspected, which struck away all security for liberty or life, and delivered over any good and innocent person to any bad and guilty one; prisons gorged with people who had committed no offence and could obtain no hearing; these things became the established order…'"

Lifting his head, he spoke to the camera again. "On the story goes as Dickens observes the excesses engaged in by mobs of undisciplined vicious self-appointed crusaders who believe they are promoting justice while they are creating chaos and widespread destruction. And is this not a repetitive story in human history? Is this not a story that began with Cain and Abel and has still not been resolved?

"Fortunately, there are other kinds of crusaders; for example, Meister Eckhart, a true man of God."

From the top shelf of the bookcase, he took an old volume with a black cover and a hardly visible title: *Men Who Have Walked With God.*

As he turned to the camera, he raised his index finger. "One moment, please." Shuffling to the scoop-back chair, he sat, and methodically flipped the pages until he found the Eckhart passage he was seeking. "This is an excerpt from one of our medieval mystic's sermons, The Eternal Birth: 'If the divine birth is to occur in a man in all its shining reality and clarity, it must flood up and out of the soul in which God is indwelling -- and that will be when all the man's own efforts are suspended, and the soul's ground left receptive to

God.'" He heaved a deep sigh.

As he closed the book, he fixed his gaze on the camera, and said, "Meister Eckhart believed, as I do, that to reach our souls we must go back to the center of our beings, away from the entanglements of life. It may seem like a contradiction that to find God we must relax, look within, and suspend all of our efforts. Instead of screaming for God to come to us, we only have to open the door and tell him he is welcome to visit us at his own convenience. That is how our paradoxical friend, God, prefers to operate, my friends. Now, after a brief message of interest to us all, we will be back with more..."

He got up, went to the bookcase, put the black book carefully on the top shelf next to the Jung volume, and bent over. Looking toward the rear of the bookcase, he asked, "Are you in there, Urda? Are you weaving your web? Waiting for your prey? I have not seen you for quite some time. Are you meditating? I have not seen Skuld either. Have you seen our flea companion? No answer. I suppose you are going through withdrawal from the material world, as I am inclined to do."

Straightening up, he took his prayer book from the top shelf, and went to the scoop-back gray plastic chair. For a while he turned the pages, pausing briefly, scanning. Then he stopped. He did not seem conscious of the cameras now.

When he started speaking the prayers aloud he was whispering, not addressing an audience. "This is what I was looking for: 'Grant that I may be ever attentive at my prayers, temperate at my meals, diligent in my employments, and constant in my good resolutions. Let my conscience be ever upright and pure, my exterior modest, my conversation edifying, and my life according to our rule.'

"Ah yes, I must be attentive at my prayers, temperate at my meals, diligent, constant, upright, pure, modest, edifying...according to the rule."

He nodded his head several times. Then he crossed

himself, saying loudly, "In the name of the Father and of the Son and of the Holy Ghost. Amen. Thank you, Father, for all of the gifts you have bestowed on me. I am content to serve you in the way you have chosen. My hermitage suits your purposes and mine very well. I have the necessities of life, my inspirational literature, my solitude."

He held his right hand up to his ear and cupped it, as if hard of hearing. "I cannot quite hear what you say to me. Yes, that is better. Now I hear you. But who are you? The Cardinal? His Eminence? Why would a Cardinal be talking to a simple monk? Honors? I am only a simple monk. A brother in The Order of The Holy Chalice. We shun identity and honors, you see.

"You say the honor is deserved and I am expected to accept? Thank you, but I am content here at the monastery. I have no wish to receive any honors...Oh, the Cardinal has gone. I have no idea why he came to see such a simple monk as I in the first place. It must have been a mistake."

He returned to his prayer book, opened it to the beginning pages, turned them slowly, stopped, and said, "The Seven Deadly Sins. Yes, they are very deadly. Pride. Covetousness. Lust. Anger. Gluttony. Envy. Sloth. But God, our constant friend, will deliver us from evil and make us virtuous. For every deadly sin there is a corresponding virtue. Humility. Liberality. Chastity. Meekness. Temperance. Brotherly love. Diligence."

He made the Sign of The Cross. "Help me to be virtuous, O Lord. Help me to perform good works, alms-deeds, or works of mercy, prayer and fasting. I have no material things to give, O Lord, but I offer you my prayers and my fasting."

He nodded and said, "I offer you my poverty, chastity, and obedience. Thank you for placing me in a monastery where it is possible for your humble servant to find contentment." He nodded his head three times, closed the prayer book, put it on his lap, crossed himself, and his eyes remained closed for several minutes.

Opening his eyes, he looked toward the black velvet wall, blinked a few times, and asked, "Who are you? Iris and Anna? That seems to hold no meaning for me. Why would two women such as you come to visit a humble monk in his hermitage?

"Oh yes, I do appreciate your contrasting beauty. Iris with your hair of the sun and Anna with your hair of fire. Iris with your eyes of blue. Anna with your eyes of emerald green. God has seen fit to endow you with heavenly attributes. Yes, you are welcome. You bring a hint of God's infinite goodness to my chamber."

He paused and listened for a while, nodding attentively. "Yes, I understand what you are saying, but I do have a question, if you will permit me to pose it. Why do I deserve your praise when I am only practicing the virtues God wishes me to practice? I need no reward for avoiding the Seven Deadly Sins.

"Virtue is its own reward. I simply have no desire to be sinful, so your special tribute is hardly deserved. In all humility, I suggest that you divert your praise to one more worthy than I...and...Oh, they are gone. Well, it was good of them to come, but I hardly deserved the praise they were bestowing on me. A simple monk needs no..."

The silvery gray spider dropped from up above and landed on the golden embossed crucifix symbol on the cover of the prayer book lying in his lap. "You startled me, Urda, coming down to me from above like that. Does your visit have some heavenly meaning?" He watched the spider walk slowly around the surface of his prayer book.

"You are welcome to wander around my prayer book, Urda. What is mine is yours. Take your time and stay a while. I have missed you. In fact, I was asking Verdandi where you had gone. You seem to have been among the missing, but I assumed that you were making a retreat in order to regain your perspective."

His hands were on his knees and remained in that position while he looked down at the spider and talked to it. "It is obvious that perspective is a problem for all of us, Urda. Even a simple monk such as I may tend to take my situation for granted, which is certainly uncalled for. How many men have the opportunity to do what they wish to do and live according to the will of God in their chosen calling?

"I am very fortunate, residing in this monastery with my solitude and my inspirational literature, the necessities of life, and periodic opportunities to spread the word of God via the electronic medium. I have much to be thankful for, as you have, also.

"Consider how fortunate you are to have such a casual orientation toward the chaos of present day civilization. Your orientation toward the past is a great gift from God, Urda, and you should be forever grateful for it. Consider how blessed you are to be spared the frenetic activity of your ant associate, Verdandi, and the restless anxiety-ridden tendencies of your flea associate, Skuld."

He paused and said nothing for a few moments as he watched Urda move her eight legs very slowly on the surface of the prayer book. Then Urda stretched her legs over the side of the book, walked onto Doctor Fayne's smock, went to the bottom edge of it, and sent a lifeline filament out of her spinnaret, letting herself down slowly to the floor where she walked slowly and directly to the bookcase. She climbed up to the top shelf, walked along the visible upper edges of the bindings; and when she reached the large black bound book titled *The Holy Bible*, she disappeared into the space between the top of the books and the top of the bookcase.

"It was considerate of you to drop in," said the deviant to Urda." I was concerned about your welfare, so it is good to know that you are well."

He was opening his prayer book again, to a section about

halfway into the book, when there was an electrical clicking sound, then a buzz, and the electrified door at the entrance to his triangular shaped triangle slid open. In stepped Sumner, in his olive green smock, his vacuum cleaner in his hand.

"Why, it is Brother Summoner. Welcome to my humble hermitage, Brother."

Sumner's drooping right eyelid raised slightly, and with the bloodshot bulging eyeball aiming at the deviant, he said, "Look, Fayne, I'm no brother of yours and my name isn't Suh-muh-ner, or whatever you're saying. It's Sumner, and that's that."

Doctor Fayne whispered, "He tends to misjudge me. I think he forgets our monastic surroundings."

Sumner's nose was twitching as he walked slowly around the triangle, looking for some bit of debris to clean up. But there was nothing to be found. Persistently though, he made a search throughout the triangle, this time even kneeling to examine corners.

"Nothing," he said as he examined the toilet where there was not one spot or stain. He went to the drain and kneeled down and poked his finger into the grating and grunted. "This place is so clean I can't stand it."

"What are you seeking, Brother Summoner?" asked the deviant. "Perhaps I might help you find whatever it is."

"I don't need help from you," replied Sumner. The Doctor nodded, focused his attention on his prayer book, and muttered to himself as he read: "Firmly convinced that the salvation of our immortal souls is the one great business of life, the purpose for which we have come into the world, we solemnly resolve for the future not only to do all in our power to avoid every grievous sin in thought, word, and deed, but also to shun every necessary occasion that might imperil our souls. We further resolve..."

Sumner was hovering over him, pointing his hand at the prayer book. "Put that loony book away, Fayne, and get up off that chair and let's get going."

The deviant asked politely, "Does Father Abbot wish to see me, or is it time for a visit with Father Confessor?"

"All I know is The Kuh...Kuh...Keeper wants to see you, and nobody keeps The Kuh...Kuh...Keeper waiting."

Doctor Fayne whispered, "He seems confused. He must mean Father Abbot when he says The Keeper. Possibly he is imbued with fervor over the biblical reference to being our brother's keeper."

He shrugged and said, "I am just about finished my prayer, Brother Summoner." He turned his attention back to the prayer book and continued: "We further resolve to fulfill with greater exactness and fidelity the duties of our station in life, to give more attention to..."

Sumner reached down and closed the prayer book with his heavy hands and said, "Enough of that bunk, Fayne. You're coming with me. The Kuh...Kuh…Keeper doesn't wait for anybody, fella."

"May I replace my prayer book in the bookcase?"

"Make it fast."

The deviant moved at his usual slow pace, replaced the book carefully on the top shelf, turned toward Sumner, and said, "I will see Father Abbot now."

The vacuum was being waved perilously close to his upper lip as Sumner instructed him, "Get going to the door, Fayne." He pointed toward the doorway. "Go right over there now. No more messing around, get me?"

The deviant went into the corridor; then the electrified door closed behind them. It was dimly lit in the somewhat dusty corridors leading to The Clean Room. And as they walked along, Sumner told him about the recent AEC-FRN military clash. When Doctor Fayne questioned him about the initials, Sumner said, "I already told you all about the initials. Don't you remember anything?"

He impatiently explained that the AEC was the Alliance

of Enterprising Countries and the FRN was the Federation of Rising Nations. Then, when he was telling the deviant about Philiston, Doctor Fayne asked, "Philiston?"

Sumner shook his head. "How many times I got to tell you about your own country, Fayne? I've never seen such a nut case as you, fella."

Sumner explained that Philiston was the capitol city of the United Econocratic Provinces, where Chairman Cashin presided over the Supreme Econocratic Council, which made all decisions affecting "the good of the economy."

Then he said curtly, "I suppose you don't even know about the Econocongress."

"The world outside my hermitage is a mystery to me, Brother Summoner."

"The Econocongress is where the big shots from The Provinces get together and discuss what's best for the economy and then they give their ideas to the Supreme Econocratic Council and they...I don't know why I'm telling you all this. You don't remember anything from one minute to the next."

The deviant replied, "I am content to know nothing of the world outside, Brother Summoner. If I ask you questions it is only out of politeness and humility. I have no need for such knowledge. So, if you feel that explaining the ways of the world to me is a pointless activity, then you may simply retain such information for your own edification and practical use. You see, I have no practical enterprises. I live only to practice virtues and abide by the will of Our Lord. Jesus, Mary, and Joseph, please pray for this thy humble servant." He nodded his head and crossed himself.

Squinting down the corridor some distance ahead of them, the deviant said, "I wonder who that is."

Sumner replied, "There's nobody there."

"Oh, yes, Brother Summoner. There is someone up ahead. She is dressed in a long, flowing robe and surrounded by a halo of light. She looks like...but it cannot be the Blessed Mother. Why would the Blessed Mother visit this humble monk? I must be mistaken."

He stopped and threw himself on his knees, still staring straight ahead. "It is you then? The Blessed Mother?" He crossed himself. Then he said very loudly, "Hail Mary, full of grace, the Lord is with thee. Blessed art thou among women, and blessed is the fruit of thy womb, Jesus."

"Get up off the floor, you psycho," ordered Sumner. "You and your idiot praying are getting on my nerves, Fayne."

Doctor Fayne said, "The Blessed Mother is gone. She told me to keep up the good work and she said..."

"Blessed Mother? What's this bunk, Fayne? Look, fella, why don't you just move along and keep that crazy talk to yourself. If you start pulling that crap when you're with The Kuh...Kuh...Keeper you're going to get your body thrown in The Trap. So get moving. We have to get you cleaned up."

They went to The Clean Room, where the Doctor thanked Sumner for the opportunity of having such a thorough shower, blessed the fresh smock and slippers, and told Sumner how contented he was with the procedures of the monastery because they all seemed to lend themselves to the greater glory of God. Then Sumner led him to The Keeper's chamber over corridors that were immaculately clean from The Clean Room entrance all the way to The Keeper's place.

"You may go now, Sumner," said The Keeper's loudly amplified voice. "Come right ahead, Doctor Fayne. Come toward my golden door."

The deviant muttered, "Yes, Father Abbot." The Keeper's door slid open. "Or is it Father Confessor?"

He stepped through the doorway and received the automated tranquilizer and memory stimulator shots. Then he threw himself on his knees on the dull golden metallic floor, crossed himself, and said, "In the name of the Father and of the Son and of the Holy..."

"Doctor Fayne!" insisted The Keeper. "How many times do I have to tell you that this is not a confessional? We no longer have ridiculous churches and confessionals in the Provinces. We have professional psychotherapy available to all citizens. Now get up on your feet and take off your slippers and put them at the edge of the oval rug."

Doctor Fayne rose slowly while nodding his head, carefully took off his slippers, and said, "It is good to bare one's feet periodically and return them to the natural state." He placed the slippers at the edge of the oval rug, threw himself on his knees, and said, "Then Job rose up, and rent his garments, and..."

"Doctor Fayne," interjected The Keeper over the amplification system. "This is not a chapel. We are a nonsectarian institution. Have I not told you that there are no more religious institutions in the Provinces? You are here to complete The Unveiling, and you would be well advised to proceed immediately, without further impulsive actions, to the set of three steps so that we may continue where we left off during our previous session."

The deviant whispered, "His memory has failed him. What else could this be but a chapel? And there is the confessional he describes as a set of three steps. Father Abbot is not quite himself today."

"I am not Father Abbot," insisted The Keeper. "Now proceed without further comment to the second step."

"As you wish," said the deviant, stepping onto the rug. Immediately his body reacted to the sensual stimulation of the rug, and he made the Sign of The Cross several times while nodding his head reverently as he continued to walk across the rug. "Lead us not into temptation," he prayed aloud. "And deliver us from evil."

"You are not being led into temptation or evil, Doctor," said The Keeper. "You are simply reacting to the sensuality of my oval rug. Proceed to the second step."

Doctor Fayne went to the steps, took the assigned position, crossed himself, and announced, "Thy will be done, O Lord." Then he put the palms of his hands together in a prayer posture.

He said, "Bless me Father, for I have sinned. I confess to almighty God, and to you, Father, that I have sinned exceedingly in thought, word, deed and omission, through my fault. It has been several weeks since my last confession, and I accuse myself of the following sins: There have been times when my disposition has not been what it should have been and..."

"Enough," insisted The Keeper. "I command you to be totally silent."

The deviant complied, staring straight ahead at the blurry golden circle in the center of the golden screen-like translucent wall. The Keeper kept him in that condition for several minutes, allowing no comments. Then, when Doctor Fayne's eyes had the glazed look, and his body began to go limp, The Keeper said, "Begin where you left off during our last session. Anna was knocking at your door, but you were not going to give her access to your quarters. Proceed."

"The look in her eyes always filled me with dread when I saw it straight on. So I hesitated before answering her knock. The change she had gone through was horrifying. Even her facial structure had changed. Each time I saw her face it left an after-image that hovered in my mind all day, no matter what I was doing.

"As I stood there that hollow-eyed look of hers kept filling my mind and I was filled with guilt for how I had rejected her, so I decided to answer the door, praying to God to forgive me and give me the strength to live with her in a new way. Yes, I prayed to God to help me accept my penance and go on with the work the Lord wanted me to do.

"When the evening meal was over, she nodded her head and said formally, 'Good Night, Doctor' as she left to go to her room. The next morning I was prepared for another similar day...she...I...she...the next morning she...then...and then..."

"Doctor!" said The Keeper firmly, "Compose yourself. The Unveiling is coming along quite well, up to now. Stay with me. Do not drift off. You are very close to the third step. Now tell me what happened the next morning."

"and then...and then..." The deviant looked confused...stroked his black-and gray beard thoughtfully, shook his head again. "and then..." He looked upward. "'O God, who dost gladden us by the annual expectation of our Redemption, grant that we, who now receive with joy Thine only-begotten Son as our Redeemer, may behold Him without fear when He comes as our judge, even the same Lord Jesus Christ Thy Son, who...'"

"Doctor, do not exasperate me," said The Keeper. "This is no place for prayers. This is a place for revealing the truth about your deviation from the norm. A place for becoming healthy. A place of rational renewal. Go on with your story."

"Yes, Father Abbot. I will go on with the story. 'And when the days of Pentecost were drawing to a close, they were all together in one place. And suddenly there came a sound from heaven, as of a violent wind blowing, and it filled the whole house where they were sitting. And there appeared to them parted tongues as of fire, which settled upon each of them. And they were all filled with the Holy Spirit and began to speak in foreign tongues, even as the Holy Spirit...'"

"Doctor Fayne, what are you doing? What story is this? Something out of The Bible?"

"Why, certainly, Father Abbot. It is from the second chapter of the Acts of the Apostles, and..."

"Enough," said The Keeper irritably. "I can see that our session has passed the point of effectiveness. Remove yourself from my chamber, Doctor. Go across the oval rug and put on your slippers."

"As you wish, Father Abbot." He nodded his head, made the Sign of The Cross, and stepped onto the rug where he was stimulated sensually, crossed himself repeatedly, and as he put on his slippers he prayed, "Lead us not into temptation but deliver us from evil. Amen."

Then he threw himself on his knees on the hard metallic floor and prayed, "Thank you, Lord, for all the Blessings you have bestowed on me."

"Go!" ordered The Keeper, "Leave without further delay. Our session has ended, Doctor."

The deviant whispered, "There must be some mistake. Father Abbot keeps calling me Doctor, but I am a simple monk, not a doctor."

Ignoring the deviant's remarks, The Keeper said, "Go to your triangle now, Doctor Fayne. Sumner will accompany you. Rise from that kneeling position and go to your triangle...and rest."

"Yes, Father Abbot. I will rejoin Brother Summoner and return to my hermitage." He got up and headed toward the door, which was sliding open. At the door he turned and looked placidly toward the blurry golden circle in the center of the translucent screen on the golden wall, and he said, "Thank you, Father Abbot. May God bless you. And please pray for me. I am going to my hermitage now, where I will rest. Rest in peace."

Case Report Disposition
Observation to be continued.

8.

Case Report
Deviant: Fayne, Wylie, Ph.D.
Number: 1
Shelter: Bentham Deviant Shelter
Province: Avernus
Housing: Total Scrutiny
Therapy: Time Void
Technique: Observation and Dialogue
Condition: To be ascertained.

Summary of Session Number 8

During my next observation of the deviant's triangle, I noted that it was as close to the nadir of filth as it had ever been. I observed that there was hardly a portion of floor that was not littered. His hair was matted and grimy. His black-and-gray beard was scraggly and included the remnants of a number of meals.

His forehead was deeply creased, and his dark brown eyes were squinting as he focused his attention, with clenched teeth, on the piece of paper in the typewriter. The ends of his lips curled up every few seconds in what was more of a grimace than a smile or frown.

"God hear my cries." This was the line he had typed about twenty times, weighing each word as if it had never been typed before. Suddenly he threw his hands up in the air, yanked the paper out of the typewriter, crumpled the page into a tight ball, stood up, held the ball of paper up to his mouth, sent three wads of spit onto it, compressed the ball still further, and rolled it between the palms of his hands with a very intense expression on his face.

Heaving the ball toward the nearest video camera, he shouted, "Up yours with a cactus!" He waved his index finger at the camera. "Tuck it up your touch hole." He leaped up from his stool, shook his fist at the camera, and then his eyes widened with horror. He clamped his hands on top of his head and began pushing down.

He screamed, "The bastards are taking my head!" One hand pressed on the top of his head, and the other waved under his chin. "My neck is gone!" he shouted. "Don't take my head!" With both hands on his head he backed into the plastic scoop-back chair and sat there for several moments muttering, "They're taking me apart, piece by piece."

He slumped down into the chair, hands still clasped on top of his head and pushing down hard. Then, stretching his long bony legs straight out in front of the chair, he lifted his right leg so the heel of his right foot rested on the toes of his left. He stayed that way for several minutes, never taking his hands from his head.

With eyes wide open, he stared straight ahead at the black velvet wall. Then his eyelids drooped, his breathing slowed, and his mouth hung open. He moved his hands rapidly from his head and they clasped his neck. Touching his face, he muttered, "They decided to let me keep my head."

He took his smock and pulled it down so it covered his knees. Then he stood up and went to the utility table where the tray was partially filled with the remains of his fish sticks, peas and mashed potatoes. Nodding his head, he went to his sink, cupped his left hand, filled it with water, went to the tray, threw the water on the food, returned to the sink again, and repeated the process several times. Then, with both hands, he blended the water, fish sticks, peas and potatoes into a soggy mess.

Turning to the camera nearest him, he heaved the food mess in that direction and shouted, "Try it. You'll like it." Then he began to walk back to the scoop-back chair, wiping his hands on his smock, and muttered, "My body is not my own. My lower parts are out on loan. I've cooked my goose. So what's the use?"

When he was almost to the chair he shouted, "Ouch. Yikes! Shit! That hurts!" He began shifting his feet from one to the other, as if walking on a bed of hot coals. Looking down, he shouted, "My God! There are hundreds of triangles with snakes crawling between them. Argh!"

He jumped in the air about a foot. "Get me out of here!" He continued to jump as he moved toward his chair. Then he climbed up, stood on the seat, and shuddered. His eyes widened in amazement. "Gone? Where did they go? Who'll ever know?"

He started to put his right foot down to the floor, but then pulled it back as fast as he could, stood on the chair seat again, and looked down. "Wolves prowling. With sharp teeth and shining eyes. Leaping around in squares and circles. Growling and leaping. No!"

He pushed with his left hand and then with his right as if trying to keep leaping animals away from his legs. Then he stopped flailing his arms. "Gone? Where did they go? Who'll ever know?"

He stood there a while, and when no other frightening visions erupted in front of him, he carefully slid down and seated himself in the scoop-back chair, looked at the velvet wall, sighed, and said angrily, "Damn snakes, wolves, triangles, circles and squares. Never any peace." He got up fast, went to the bookcase, pushed aside the soiled copies of Goethe's *Faust* and *The Basic Writings of Sigmund Freud*, then grabbed the clean white-covered book with the red and black lettering: *The Prince*, by Machiavelli.

When he was seated, he looked at the front cover and asked, "What's the good word, Niccolo?" The vertical crease in the center of his forehead deepened as he squinted at the cover. "Power. Yes. That's the ticket, Niccolo."

He held the book in his left hand, took his right thumb, jammed it into the pages at random, and began to read: "'...the experience of our times shows those princes to have done great things who have had little regard for good faith, and have been able by astuteness to confuse men's brains, and who have ultimately overcome those who have made loyalty their foundation.'"

"Ah-hah. The slippery bastard knows the score: 'You must know, then, that there are two methods of fighting, the one by law the other by force: the first method is that of men, the second of beasts; but as the first method is often insufficient, one must have recourse to the second. It is therefore necessary for a prince to know well how to use both the beast and the man. This was covertly taught to rulers by ancient writers.'"

He looked up at the nearest camera. "Ah-hah. They all studied the same book, didn't they?"

Nodding his head several times, he muttered, "So that's your good word, Niccolo, right here in the book: 'A prince being thus obliged to know well how to act as a beast must imitate the fox and the lion, for the lion cannot protect himself from traps, and the fox cannot defend himself from wolves. One must therefore be a fox to recognize traps, and a lion to frighten wolves. Those that wish to be only lions do not understand.

"'Therefore, a prudent ruler ought not to keep faith when by so doing it would be against his interest, and when the reasons which made him bind himself no longer exist. If men were all good, this precept would not be a good one; but as they are bad, and would not observe their faith with you, so you are not bound to keep faith with them.'"

"Ah-hah! You tell them, Niccolo. Tell them how to connive and stay alive when they arrive--instead of getting knived."

He slammed the book shut, took his thumb, jammed it into a section near the end of the book, opened to it, and read, "'Men will always be false to you unless they are compelled by necessity to be true.'" He slammed the book shut again, jammed his right thumb into an early section of the book, and read, "'It must be noted that men must either be caressed or else annihilated; they will revenge themselves for small injuries, but cannot do so for great ones; the injury therefore that we do to a man must be such that we need not fear his vengeance.'"

He jammed his thumb into the pages again, and read, "'One ought to be both feared and loved, but as it is difficult for the two to go together, it is much safer to be feared than loved.' Ah-hah!" He looked up at the cameras. "You bastards memorized this stuff, right?" He scaled the book up at the camera. "Well, swallow this, you creeps!"

The book went into an arc, missed the camera, and landed in a puddle of fresh urine near the foot of his bed. He extended his middle finger at the camera nearest him, waved it several times in a circular motion and shouted, "Up your Machiavelli with a rusty nickelodeon!"

Sighing, he slumped back into the chair, with his head resting on the top of the hard plastic backrest. As he began to close his eyes, they popped open wide and he asked, "Who? Mrs. Turnbull? I don't know any Mrs. Turnbull. I disobeyed you? I stayed in the cellar too long?"

"Ow!" He flinched as if he had just received a slap on his left cheek. "Damn it, I wasn't pounding off down there. I was...Ouch! I didn't mean to swear. Yes, I apologize. No, please don't make me use the alcohol on it again. I promise on The Bible that I won't do it again. Just don't...she's gone. Here a minute, there a minute, everywhere a minute. Bore a hole, bore a hole, right through the sugar bowl."

Lifting his smock, he took his index finger and made a circular motion with the tip of his finger, using his navel for the center of the circle. "Bore a hole, bore a hole, right through the sugar bowl." Over and over, for several minutes, he repeated this phrase, always accompanied by the same motion of index finger around navel.

He stopped and sat silently, hands folded in his lap, lightly tapping his thumbs together. Then he clapped his hands, and sat up straight. "Mors stupebit et natura, cum resurget creatura, judicanti responsura...Death is struck, and nature quaking, all creation is awaking -- to its Judge an answer making.

"Judex ergo cum sedebit, quidquid latet apparebit: Nil inultum remanebit ...When the Judge His seat attaineth, and each hidden deed arraigneth, nothing unavenged remaineth." He started clapping his hands together and shouted, "Mors stupebit! Judex ergo. Mors stupebit! Judex ergo! Mors..."

He stopped clapping, and said in a very solemn voice, "'Thus spake The Lord our God...Who raiseth up the needy from the earth...and lifteth the poor out of the dunghill.'" He nodded his head.

"The dunghill, the dunghill, who'll go up the dunghill? I know who. Jack and Jill. They'll go up the dunghill. Jack and Jill went up the hill, to fetch a pail of water. Jack fell down and broke his crown, and Jill came tumbling after. Then up Jack got and off did trot, as fast as he could caper. Ah hah! Up he got, as fast as he could trot, and planned to pull a caper. Up he got. Trot, trot, trot."

He shook his head. "No, no. The dunghill's got to go. It's bad news and it gives me the blues. I've been had and I've been so sad." He began to sob, then tears filled his eyes, and he said, "The blubberheads won't get off my back, or off my front. They're giving me a bellyful, trying to make me bite the dust. But I've got crust. In that I trust.

"Crust, crust, crust." For several minutes he repeated the word like a chant. Then he stopped and looked furtively around the triangle and said, "Find it. Yes, I'll find it. And I'll erase it...before it erases me." He got up slowly and began tiptoeing through the filth he had created earlier, and he squinted as he methodically examined every section of his triangle. Then he looked into the lower shelf of his bookcase.

His eyes widened and he whispered softly, "There you are, you schemer, planning to erase me as they fitted you out to do. But I'll erase you first, my bitchy little nemesis."

The red ant was scurrying in the shadowy rear of the lower shelf while Doctor Fayne remained motionless, waiting for the right instant. He watched his prey without blinking an eye, for several moments. Then the ant began moving across the lighter area in the front of the bottom shelf, near Freud's and Goethe's works.

Doctor Fayne's jaws tightened as he concentrated on the task at hand, and the muscles under his cheeks rippled. "Whack!" The ant was immobilized by the right palm of the deviant's smashing hand.

Examining the still red ant, he said aloud, "Poisoned head that I did dread, I caught your plot, now you're a blot. Your shameful deed was born from greed. You longed to see the death of me. From me in dread you often fled. Your venom swelled from hate unquelled. You learned your skill in schemes to kill. Without a doubt I've turned you out."

With his index finger he flicked the red ant into the darkness at the rear of the bottom shelf. Then he went back to the scoop-back chair, waved his middle finger at the video camera nearest him, and shouted, "You know that ant you sent to me? With that special poison? He's had a little accident. He's what you might call...diverted from his mission. Try again, you bastards. Maybe you'll be...Argh!"

His face contorted in pain and his hands flew up and clamped the right side of his head."Hrgh! Ooh! Ah! The pounding. Oh, the rotten pounding." For a few minutes he repeated this scene, first with one side of his head, then the other. Finally, he vomited all over himself and then slumped back in the chair and breathed heavily with closed eyes.

He seemed to be sleeping despite the discomfort and stench of his vomit. Then he grunted and his eyes opened wide. He tipped his head toward the left, as if trying to hear a faint voice more clearly, and said, "What the hell is that noise? Squeak-squeak. Squeak-squeak. Springs? A bed? Is that what it is? A bed squeaking? Squeak-squeak. Squeak"

He held his hands over his ears and shook his head as if trying to get the sounds out of it, and then he shouted, "Turn it off, you bastards!" His eyes looked at the floor in horror, and he pulled his legs up onto the chair and sat Indian fashion, staring down at the floor. "Blood! Covered with blood! Right up there..."

He looked up at the ceiling and shouted, "That's where it's coming from. My God, it looks like a huge pecker ripped from someone's body...and it's dripping and filling up this place...and there's this hand holding it. Now I see a woman with a white dress and a face like an animal. It's a wolf, with snarling teeth bared, drooling, with hate in her moonlit eyes.

"Now she's squeezing it with both hands and more blood's coming down and it's raining blood on me now!" He started flailing his hands all over his body, as if trying to push away the shower of blood, and he leaped up so that he was standing on the chair, shaking with fear.

There was a click and a buzz and the door to his triangle slid open. His attendant, sniffing the triangular place, looked at Doctor Fayne and asked, "What are you doing up on the chair, Fayne? You trying to find a way out of this place? Well, there's no way out, so forget it."

The deviant blinked his eyes, shook his head, and looked at his sallow faced attendant, saying, "The blood...the blood! It's all over the...it's...it's gone now. It came down in buckets and now it's gone. Here a drop, there a drop, everywhere a drop-drop. Here a drop, there a drop, everywhere a drop."

"Get your body off that chair, Fayne. You're coming with me to see The Kuh...Kuh...Keeper." He was sniffing as he approached the deviant. "The Kuh...Kuh...Keeper doesn't like any... oh-oh!" There was a hissing sound and Sumner looked up and said, "Yup, the shower is coming on."

Sumner ran toward the door and leaped into the corridor just as the cleaning shower heads emitted their high pressure streams of chemically treated water throughout the triangle, thoroughly drenching the place, then spinning Doctor Fayne around in his scoop-back chair until everything was soaked, including him and the damp pile of residue that was near the drain after the cleaning process had ended.

Then the forced hot air ducts filled the chamber with heat and dried everything that had been wet, including Doctor Fayne. "Now they'll sauna me to death!" he shouted in between gasps of breath. "They know heat's my enemy!"

Sumner came back into the triangle, sniffing. Then he shook his head. The short, broad-shouldered attendant went to the pile of residue near the drain, put his vacuum down, shook his head, and muttered, "Hardly anything in this whole place for me to clean." He shook his head as he picked up the Machiavelli book and returned it to the lower shelf of the book case. Then he dumped the refuse into the waste bin.

With his vacuum, he went over to Doctor Fayne and ordered, "Get your body moving because The Kuh...Kuh...Keeper won't wait for anybody."

He pointed his finger toward Doctor Fayne's face and waved it menacingly. "Maybe you need a little help to get you moving, huh Fayne?"

The deviant stood up. Then he turned to Sumner. "Who the hell are you? And where did you come from?"

"I'm Sumner, and don't give me that bunk, Fayne, making like you don't know me." He shook his head in disbelief. "I'm not one of those people that was born yesterday, you know. I'm your attendant. Don't tell me you don't know me."

"Slumner? Is that you? My attendant? You' re no attendant. They sent you to kill me with that vicious thing." He pointed to the vacuum cleaner.

"The name isn't Slumner, it's Sumner, and this only cleans things up after you make your messes. When I need to, a wave of my hand activates your implants and that gets you moving. Look, your own behavior gives you your pain."

The deviant grimaced and held his hands on his ears. "Can't you make that whining nasal voice of yours work a little softer?"

"There is no way I can change how I talk, Fayne, anymore than you can change how screwed up you are. Now, get your body moving!"

Doctor Fayne took his hands from his ears. "What choice do I have, you body-reaming sadistic moron?"

"You have no choice, Fayne."

"You said it, Slumner." He mimicked the nasal whine. "I have no choice."

"Make fun of me, Fayne, and you're wasting your time. It doesn't affect me. Now get moving down the corridor to The Clean Room." He pointed.

"Right, Slumner. Since you're so polite, why not?"

He walked toward the door which was now sliding open. Then he suddenly turned toward the dart board, took the three friction-head darts, held them out to Sumner, and said, "How's about a game?"

"I don't play games, Fayne."

"Well, I do." said the deviant, heaving the three darts at Sumner's face and hitting him on the cheeks and forehead. "Up yours, you creep!" The Doctor started running into the corridor. "How about a race? Can you keep up the pace?"

He began running along the corridor, and when Sumner's heavy footsteps started to echo behind him the deviant kicked off his slippers and ran barefoot along the cement floors of the dull gray corridor. His bare feet slapped as he ran, and Sumner's heavy tread thumped a short distance behind him.

Soon Sumner's whining voice came at the back of his head. "Your body is going to end up in The Trap, Fayne."

"Shove your Trap!" shouted the deviant over his shoulder

as he ran. By the time he got within sight of The Clean Room door, he was panting heavily, and the gap between the pat of his bare feet and the thump of Sumner's feet had shrunk. Then Sumner's whining voice threatened, "You asked for it, nut case, so now you're going to get it."

The implants were activated by a wave of Sumner's hand, throwing the deviant to the floor. "Hrgh! Arghl" The Doctor's eyes were still closed as he grunted from the electric shocks on just about every part of his body. His body heaved each time Sumner waved. Then his eyes opened and as he looked up at Sumner's parrot-nosed, drooping-eyed face, horror covered his own face.

Then Sumner yanked up the lower part of the deviant's gray smock, exposed the genitals, and muttered, "Now you'll see what happens when you go and screw around with Sumner, nut case."

The hand waved and the electricity entered the deviant's scrotum sending his whole body into spasms. He screamed at the top of his lungs incoherently as Sumner stood back and waited. The spasms stopped finally and the deviant lay there on his back on the floor, completely limp, naked from his waist down.

Sumner moved his hand very slowly toward the deviant's genitals, and the Doctor began to shake. "No more. Please! No more."

"Are you going to knock off the crap, Fayne?"

"Right, no more crap. Anything you say, Slumner."

"Then get your body up and into The Clean Room, or The Kuh...Kuh...Keeper's going to throw your body into The Trap. Maybe after what he just saw you do, that's what's going to happen to you anyways."

Sumner activated the lock-switch, and the door to The Clean Room opened. The deviant shivered, but said nothing as he went into the room. Then, as ordered, a more compliant deviant took off his smock and put it into a dirty clothes bin, extended his arm for a shot of blue tranquilizer solution from Sumner's medication gun, got into one of the series of coffee-cup shaped mesh baskets, and was transported through the washing process.

After being soaped, pummeled with whirling brushes, rinsed and forced-air dried, Sumner told him to put on a clean smock and slippers, and led him to the corridor again.

As they walked along the corridor, Doctor Fayne said, "You're a ball busting bastard."

"That kind of talk doesn't bother me, Fayne. If you know what's good for you, you'll just move forward and not try to run away. Or you know what."

The deviant's vulgar frame of mind seemed to intensify as he became more and more insulting to his attendant. "Go suck yourself," he said. "Up your nose with a thorny rose, Slumner, and up your body with broken glass."

"What a screwed-up nut case you are, Fayne." Sumner lowered his voice to a whisper. "How come they put you in the Total Scrutiny set-up, Fayne? What did you do, huh?"

"Ask me no questions and I'll tell you no lies. Ask me no questions and you'll be very wise." He looked up at the video camera overhead, a short distance from him. "Up yours," he shouted, waving his middle finger at the equipment. "Up yours with a digital reproduction."

"You aren't exactly helping yourself by doing that to the cameras, Fayne."

"Shove the cameras! Up their lenses! Up their tripods! What the hell is the difference what I do? My goose is cooked. Or is my cook goosed? Get off my back, Slumner. Go cook your own goose, or goose your own cook. Drink your juice. Juice your drink. Eat your stuff. Stuff your eats. Whip your cream. Cream your whip. Feel your peel. Peel your feel. Now you're ready for another meal."

"You better knock off that rhyming bunk when you see The Kuh...Kuh...Keeper, Fayne. He doesn't like any fooling around."

"They can shove their Keeper up their floodgate! Thanks to The Keeper, I've been flayed and parlayed. I've been screwed, blued and tattooed. I've had the barbed shaft rammed up my rectum till it's raw. I've been steamed, creamed, and unseamed. I've been shucked, plucked, and clucked. I've been..."

"I think you're asking for The Trap, Fayne, and I think that's what you'll get..."

"Go pound rock salt up your body!"

"I never saw such a screwed-up nut case."

"Go shove your head up your own asshole."

The continuing vulgarity was interrupted by a slight rumbling noise, and an almost undetectable vibration went through the concrete under their feet.

Sumner said, "The damn bomb-tossers must be at it again in New Grafton. It's them FRN sympathizers, and maybe some spies. The other day they were saying spies were stirring up trouble. They don't know enough to mind their own business. They keep making waves, Fayne, sort of like you. Screwed-up nut cases, that's what they are. I'll probably be getting a bunch of them from the Patho Shelter pretty soon, for cleaning up so they can experiment with them or ship them off to the war."

"They ought to ship you off to the damn war, Slumner. You'd scare the enemy right off the battlefield. One look at you is all it would take."

"Look, Fayne. That talk doesn't bother me. Just keep moving, that's all. Do what I tell you and I won't activate the electrical impulses."

"Right, Slumner. I'll just keep moving." He nodded his head in an exaggerated way. "You said it, Slumner. Just keep...Who the hell are you? Sister who?" He stopped in his tracks, and his eyes widened as he looked straight ahead.

"Just plain Sister? You're a nun? You think I know you? I

never locked you up. Why would I lock you up? I've never locked anybody up. I'm the one who's locked up. Look right behind me and you'll see my jailer with his keys, Sister." He pointed over his shoulder.

"I'm no jailer, Fayne, and this isn't a jail. It's the Psycho Deviant Shelter in Bentham and we're just here to help you become very healthy, that's all."

"Listen to him, Sister. He's helping me become healthy. In other words, he's helping me become dead."

"Get moving, Fayne. I've had enough of your bunk."

"But Sister wants to talk, Slumner. She...Ouch! Yikes!"

Sumner had waved his hand, and Sister or no Sister, the deviant was leaping along the corridor, trembling as he went.

"Never mind the Sister bunk," said Sumner. "Just keep moving. That's all I require. The point is that The Kuh...Kuh...Keeper doesn't wait for anybody."

"Right, Slumner. The Keeper doesn't wait for anybody. Finders Keepers. Losers weepers. Humpty Dumpty sat on a wall. Humpty Dumpty had a great fall. All the King's horses and all the King's men...couldn't put Humpty together again."

He looked down as he walked along. Then he began waving his arms toward his legs and shouted, "My legs are gone. They cut them off!" As he walked, he kept looking down every couple of seconds.

Sumner's voice came at him from the rear. "If they cut your legs off, Fayne, what do you think you're walking on, huh?"

Doctor Fayne did not acknowledge Sumner's question, continued to repeat the same phrase over and over, and then suddenly shifted into a song: "I went to the animal fair...the birds and the bees were there...the big baboon...fell on his tune..." He stopped and shook his head.

"Nope, that's not part of the verse. Let's see now. Well, anyhow...at least I've got the end of it: The monkey he got drunk...sat on the elephant's trunk...the elephant sneezed...and fell on his knees...and that was the end of the monk...the monk...that was the end of the monk. That's it, Slumner. Come on and sing along! That was the end of the monk...the monk...that was the end of the monk. One more time! That was the end of the monk...the monk... "

They reached the short corridor leading to The Keeper's chamber, and Sumner ordered him to go down that brief walkway to the right. But the deviant hesitated, then turned with tears streaming down his face, and he said, "Don't you understand, Slumner? It was the end of the monk. The elephant sneezed and fell on his knees...and that was the end of the monk...the monk...that was the end..."

"You make no sense, Fayne." He pointed at the deviant's nose. "The Kuh...Kuh...Keeper doesn't like anybody making him wait, Fayne, so get moving."

From the amplifier above The Keeper's door came a loudly reverberating message: "You may go now, Sumner. Come right ahead, Doctor Fayne, toward my golden door."

The deviant, tears still streaming down his cheeks, turned again to Sumner and asked, "Don't you understand? Don't you get it, you creep? That was the end of the monk...the monk...that was...Huh! Argh! Mmm! Oh!" The implants were giving him a clear electrical message, which induced him to follow The Keeper's orders.

The sliding door clicked and buzzed and hummed as it opened. He received his shots and slowly stepped inside onto the hygienically clean, dull gold metallic floor. The Keeper said, "Come right ahead, Doctor. I have been waiting."

"I bet you have," muttered Doctor Fayne, moving ahead about two short steps and then stopping with his hands on his hips, looking defiantly at the blurry golden circle in the center of the translucent golden screen-like wall.

The Keeper said, "Take your attention away from the golden wall and remove your slippers and put them neatly on the floor next to the rug."

The deviant shook his head. "If you want my slippers off, you'd better take them off yourself."

The Keeper said, "I am ordering you to go to the edge with your slippers and place them where I instructed you to."

"Who do you think you are, bossing me around? I won't take them off." Doctor Fayne said the words very calmly, but in a rebellious tone.

When the words, amplified many times, came roaring back into his ears he gritted his teeth in pain, threw his hands over his ears as if trying to seal out the noise of his own words, and a steady outpouring of tears came streaming down his cheeks. "...take them off... take them off..."

The amplifier finally died down and The Keeper ordered, "Now take your slippers off, Doctor Fayne. Do not defy me. I am here to help you. Remember who you are, Doctor. You are a citizen of the United Econocratic Provinces, a nation whose motto is: HUMANELY DEDICATED TO HIGH QUALITY ECONOMIC LIFE FOR ALL CITIZENS.

"Here at the new Psychological Deviant Shelter in Bentham, we are dedicated to providing high quality shelter to those members of our economy who need assistance in resolving their deviations from the acceptable norm. As you know, our motto here is: WE ARE CONCERNED. You see, we want to help you become very healthy. We want to bring you to your full economic potential. So please cooperate."

"Cooperate? When the elephant sneezed and fell on his knees and snuffed out the life of the monk...the monk...was the monkey cooperating? Was he supposed to tell the elephant to come right down on him and wipe him out?"

"You are trying my patience, Doctor Fayne. Please desist from these references to elephants and monkeys, and remove your slippers as I requested."

The deviant nodded. "A great idea. Want me to sharpen the knife too? Or load the revolver? Or throw the switch at my own electrocution? Then I'll be helping to wipe myself out and cooperating with the health of the economy, right? You can say I terminated myself, isn't that it?"

"Doctor, do not press your luck. You acted quite foolishly with Sumner on the way to my chamber, and you are acting foolishly now. All you have to do is cooperate and we will get along harmoniously. We are not here to punish you. We are here to help you. Any pain you receive is not to be viewed as punishment. It is simply a motivational tool that we utilize in your rehabilitation program when other methods are not successful. Now I am giving you advance notice that soon you will receive a powerful motivational charge if you do not remove your slippers and place them at the edge of the gold oval rug."

Doctor Fayne nodded his head, and his eyes seemed to be getting the glazed look now. "Yes. Remove the slippers." He took his slippers off very slowly, went to the edge of the rug, leaned over, then suddenly leaped up to a throwing position and heaved the slippers at the blurry golden circle. Instantly, they came back at him at such a rate of speed that he was knocked to the floor with a thud. When he rose, he was dazed. Then the calming drugs set in and he became much more compliant.

The Keeper ordered him to the second of the three steps. Then, as he crossed the rug his mood shifted. He threw himself down onto the fabric and was greeted with a new electrical impulse which shocked him back to compliance. Soon he was in place on the second step, with a glazed look in his eyes and his chin resting on his arms on the rail.

The Keeper told him to carry on where he had left off in the previous session, reminding him where that had been. Then Doctor Fayne said, "Yes, I was discussing the changes in Anna. Frightening changes. And this was happening when society and government were changing drastically. More and more the phrase 'for the good of the economy' was used to justify every action of government, business, labor, education, and even The Church. The word 'economy' had taken on the various shades of meaning that the word God had once signified. In fact, belief in the economy slowly but surely became more strong than any belief in God.

"The Planned Period of Public Pleasure was followed by The Period of Financial Chaos that had humbled the expanding middle class. Then came The Period of Accommodation and The Period of Consolidation, keeping the people busy with revised power structures throughout society. And finally it was time for the Declaration of Total Econocracy: 'For the good of the economy.'

"Over and over that phrase was used, and it was soon the most widely used stock phrase in world history. It became the measure of reality and morality. It was raised to the level of an art form by the power structure, becoming the way to keep the average citizen in a state of anxiety that could only be alleviated by government action. And the rumors about impending threats were seldom specific. The power of these rumors was in their vagueness.

"'Unidentified sources have indicated that the enemy is engaging in espionage.' 'The FRN is threatening our total annihilation.' 'The FRN is building up strength for an offensive.'

"There was a distinct pattern to the rumor process. The theme was always very important and the message was always ambiguous. There were seldom any concrete facts or figures. People were left in a state of fear or hatred by the negative rumors and left anxious by the positive rumors. Also, there was a steady stream of victorious statements about actions taken in Philiston.

"National and international status reports were constantly reported. 'The economy is on an upward swing.' 'New heights of prosperity are in the offing.' 'The Alliance of Enterprising Countries has uncovered a network of FRN insurgents.' 'The AEC has beaten back the FRN offensive.'

"Rumor on top of rumor. That was how the power structure manipulated the masses. Machiavelli would have been pleased as power became the... "

The Keeper asserted, "Enough, Doctor! I am fully aware of our economic history. Please do not insult my intelligence by lecturing me on subjects in which I am thoroughly conversant. We have just one interest here, Doctor. It is to help you to become very healthy. To do this, we must complete The Unveiling. Now that I have your time reference in the early portion of The Period of Consolidation, please continue where you left off when I interrupted you. Tell me more about your relationship with Anna."

"The relationship became very destructive. From day to day she shifted personalities. One day it was the conservative but intense social worker. The next it might be the pleasure addict. The third day it would be the abandoned angry bride. And often she played the role of the depressed widow.

"It reached the point where I was torn between the choices of recommending that Anna be admitted into a rehabilitation facility, or accepting the daily torture. For a time I decided to accept the torture. I felt I had to accept it for my salvation, to atone for my sins, to be forgiven. Yes. I decided to accept it as my penance.

"The cycle of her madness went on...and on...and there were times when I believed I was as insane as she was. You see, each of the four Anna's was a distinct personality even though I knew they were one and the same person with a severely fractured mind.

"Each of them affected me in a different way. The more time I spent with them, the more aware I became of the various segments of my own personality and the more I questioned my own identity. Then a gradual change began to take place in Anna the depressed widow. As the intensity of her anguish increased, it left the plateau of emotion where it had rested for so long and Anna the widow in her black mourning dress became so tormented that her facial structure actually began to take on a new shape.

"This was no figment of my imagination. Her face actually took on the look of a demonic being, and she...demonic...she became demonic...her face became monstrous with hatred...her face...her hatred...her..."

"Doctor Fayne," insisted The Keeper, "please cease the repetition. We need to continue with The Unveiling! Proceed now, please."

"and then... and then... and then...tiber scriptus proferetur, In quo tuum continetur, Unde mundus judicetur...Lo, the book, exactly worded, Wherein all hath been recorded-- Thence shall judgment be awarded."

"Doctor! You must cease this lapse into that dead Latin language of yours which is a throwback to your absurd Catholic higher education. I command you to get back on the track of our discussion. Continue. And do not use Latin."

The glazed look was gone from the Doctor's eyes now, and replaced by a look of terror mixed with confusion. "Ingemisco tanquam reus, Culpa rubet vultus meus; Supplicanti parce, Deus...Guilty now I pour my moaning, All my shame with anguish owning: Spare, O God, Thy suppliant groaning."

"Doctor Fayne, you must proceed with The Unveiling. Rid yourself of this ridiculous tendency to drift off into Latin. Continue now."

The deviant looked toward the blurry golden circle in the center of the golden screen-like translucent wall, and he said, "Oro supplexet acclinis. Cor contritum quasi cinis. Gere curam mei finis...Low I kneel, with heart submission; See, like ashes, my contrition--Help me in my last ambition."

"Enough, Doctor. Obviously the session is over and I would be wasting my time were I to attempt to continue. I am going to move you to the third step soon, Doctor, and you are almost there. Perhaps in our next session, the truth of your comments will elevate you to that step. For now, you have my permission to cross the oval velvet rug and put on your pair of slippers and return to your triangle."

Doctor Fayne remained in place, still kneeling, still staring at the blurry golden circle. "Did you say truth? Or was it tooth? That's it. If you want to find truth, you go to the root of the tooth...like a sleuth in search of a runaway youth...who was so uncouth...that he..."

"Please do not rhyme in my chamber, Doctor. It offends my sense of propriety. Cross the oval rug and put on your slippers. Go now."

The deviant did not move. Instead he acted as if he had not heard The Keeper. "Uncouth," he muttered. "What rhymes with uncouth? Forsooth? Ruth? Booth? ...in search of a runaway youth...who was so uncouth...that he picked his nose... and shit on his clothes in a..."

"Go to your pair of slippers immediately, Doctor, or your own inner resistance will stimulate and motivate you with a burst of electricity!"

"Motivate? It's much too late...to motivate...this profligate...second-rate...poet-laureate...I'm too sedate...to salivate...or copulate...or titillate...or...Argh! Hrgh!" His hands froze to the armrest as the electricity coursed through him, sending him into a series of convulsions. "Ooh! Aah! Hrgh! Argh!"

When the jolt of electrical current had subsided, The Keeper warned him not to rhyme again, and Doctor Fayne nodded, then rose to leave the steps. When his feet touched the plush oval rug the stimulation took him into an ecstasy and he removed his smock, threw himself on the rug, and rolled back and forth in a side-to-side motion, all the while muttering, "I've got it now. This is it. I've got it now. This is it...This is it..."

"Rise, Doctor. I warn you. I will not tolerate any more delays in your departure from my chamber. Rise and go to your slippers and put them on."

The deviant hesitated for a moment. Then he shrugged his shoulders and went to his slippers muttering, "This is the unseen bastard's way of killing me. This is the prick's way of wiping me out. This is..."

The Keeper interrupted him. "I am not killing you, Doctor Fayne. You resist understanding that as your Keeper, I am helping you. I am concerned about you. I am your therapist and your friend. I am here to help you become very healthy, to normalize you, to return you to society as a contributor to the economy. The motto of this shelter is 'WE ARE CONCERNED.'"

The deviant, at the edge of the rug near his slippers, turned toward the translucent wall, clasped his left hand around his right bicep, raised his forearm and shouted, "Shove your shelter!" He extended his middle finger. "Shove your economy!" He waved his middle finger. "Shove your society!"

The third epithet came back at him, amplified many times, and pounded into his eardrums. He threw his hands up and covered his ears, clenching his teeth as tears poured down his cheeks from the intensity of the pain. He grunted and groaned. Then the echoing amplification tapered off, and finally stopped. He stood there shuddering from the experience.

"Why do you inflict such pain on yourself, Doctor? Why do you reject harmony and opt for dissidence? Why do you prefer conflict to cooperation?"

Doctor Fayne, still shuddering, asked, "Did you say cooperation? Or was it co-optation? Conflagration? Congregation? There's a congregation in this nation ...that's concerned with liquidation...not to mention usurpation... they've had their fill of vulcanization... they're in the mood for retaliation...they'll take the risk of mutilation...if that's the route to their salvation. Beware the wrath of quiet masses...not so much the working classes...but those who are sitting on their asses...tipping glasses...lads and lasses..."

"Put on your slippers," ordered The Keeper. "Enough of this inane babbling. If you want to babble on, do it in your own triangle. Put your slippers on now, or you will pay the price for your lack of cooperation. Do it now."

The deviant slowly put on his slippers, making each move in a style very much resembling motion picture slow-motion.

The Keeper said, "Go to your triangle now, and rest."

"Yes, I'll go to my triangle now, and rest. Rest in peace."
With that, he rejoined his attendant in the corridor.

Case Report Disposition
Observation to be continued.

9

Case Report
Deviant: Fayne, Wylie, Ph.D.
Number: 1
Shelter: Bentham Deviant Shelter
Province: Avernus
Housing: Total Scrutiny
Therapy: Time Void
Technique: Observation and Dialogue
Condition: To be ascertained.

Summary of Session Number 9

As I began my observation of the deviant, he was sitting erectly in the scoop-back chair and was the picture of neatness. Not a wrinkle could be found in his gray smock. His feet were planted flat on the floor. His arms were resting on the edges of the chair and the palms of his hands were facing upward as they lay limply on his legs, just above his knees. His dark brown eyes were squinting down toward his left hand as he looked with concentration at the motionless silvery spider resting there.

"Tell me, Urda," said Doctor Fayne softly. "Where have our colleagues gone? What has happened to Verdandi, our scurrying ant? What has become of Skuld, our endlessly leaping flea? It has been a very long time, it seems to me, since I have seen them in my hermitage. Have they left the monastery, leaving only you and me behind to meditate and contemplate and pray?"

The spider walked slowly to the edge of the left hand, then stepped onto an almost invisible bridge of webbing that led to the right hand, and paused in the middle of the right palm, near the parallel creases of Doctor Fayne's skin. "I could never quite understand Verdandi's scurrying, nor could I relate to Skuld's leaping. I am more inclined to think that you have the right idea, Urda.

"Your orientation to the past has much merit. Verdandi, our anxious scurrying ant, never seemed to find what he was looking for in the present, and Skuld, our leaping flea, no matter how much leaping prowess he developed, never could control his future, could he? As for myself, Urda, I have come to this monastery because the myths and fictions of social life held no value for me. In fact, they were making a spiritual life just about impossible. Here in my hermitage I am closer to The Lord."

He nodded his head and paused for a moment. "Yes, Urda, I am fortunate to have my hermitage. I am quite content here. I am more comfortable with solitude than with the bustle of contemporary life. You see, Urda, the hustle and bustle go against my nature. The others can have their action for action's sake. That gives me no satisfaction. Being closer to The Lord is what brings me satisfaction."

Pausing again for a moment, he shook his head. "No, Urda, the scurrying of the present era holds no appeal for me, and the eventual future of society as it is now constituted is bound to hold less appeal for me than the present state of affairs. So I have retreated to this hermitage to hide myself away from the scurrying and the leaping so I may have a better relationship with my inner self and with The Lord. You know, Urda, in spite of their scurrying and leaping, I miss Verdandi and Skuld. But not nearly as much as I would miss you if you were to go."

The spider began to move to the edge of the palm of his right hand and then hesitated. "Have I said something to offend you, Urda?" asked Doctor Fayne, the vertical furrow in his brow deepening with concern. "Have I embarrassed you by saying that I appreciate your companionship? Does that offend your sense of independence? If so, I beg your forgiveness."

The spider moved from his hand down to his leg, then

dropped on a silken thread to the floor and went in a straight line to the bookcase, climbed to the lower shelf, and began circling aimlessly on the soiled edges of the three books by Goethe, Freud, and Machiavelli. The circling was in fits and starts, not in the usual methodical style of the spider.

Then, after a few moments of this erratic behavior, the spider darted off the three volumes, went in a straight line along the lower shelf, and climbed to the top shelf, up the green-and-white binding of Jung's *Modern Man In Search Of A Soul*. Then it disappeared into the darkness between the tip of the gray plastic bookcase and the tops of the books on the upper shelf.

"You are welcome anytime, Urda," he said after the spider had gone out of his line of sight. "It is always a pleasure to see you."

He turned and sat erectly in the scoop-back chair, stroked his black and gray beard a few times, nodded thoughtfully, and looked up at the nearest video camera. He threw up his hands and a slight smile came to his lips as he said to the camera, "The time has come again, my friends, for our brief period of contemplation on the wisdom of the ages." He rose from the chair slowly, with his eyes still fixed on the camera, and said, "Our thought for today, by the way, is 'God is our loving Father.'"

Turning, he headed for the bookcase, explaining to the camera that he was about to read passages from four different texts. Taking the four texts from the top shelf and not disturbing the Jung volume on which the spider had last been seen, he returned to the scoop-back chair, and stacked the four books in his lap. On top was a maroon volume with gold lettering: *The Teaching of The Catholic Church*.

He methodically searched the pages, and near the end of the book he stopped and said, "Here we are." He began to read. "'In Heaven the Blessed will see all things in God and God in all things. They will see all things in that divine order in which they stand in God's mind. Their place and position in the universe that God created will be understood, for the outlook of the Saints on all things will resemble that of God.'" He nodded. "Think about those words, my good people."

He tilted his head in an attitude of pleading to the camera as he lifted the other three books, put the maroon one at the bottom of the pile, and opened a black bound book with gold lettering on it. The book was titled *Men Who Have Walked With God*. He flipped the pages to the middle of the book, then turned several pages carefully and spoke to the camera.

"We have discussed Meister Eckhart before and you will recall that the Prior was a very sober philosopher. He truly believed that God is our loving Father. 'Nothing is as close to me as God,' he says. 'He is nearer to me than I am to my self. His presence is my being.'" He spoke directly to the camera. "What a friend of God the Prior was."

Closing that book, he put it at the bottom of the pile of four books, and took the blue-bound volume from the top, *The Phenomenon of Man*, by Teilhard de Chardin. He flipped the pages near the back, then fingered them carefully until he had found what he was after.

"Listen to what our Jesuit says to us. After noting that Christianity is more necessary to our modern world than ever before, he says, 'In one manner or another it still remains true that, even in the view of the mere biologist, the human epic resembles nothing so much as a way of the Cross.' Think of that, my friends, and offer your sufferings and your failures up to God, who knows what is best for us."

Closing that book, he put it at the bottom of the pile in his lap. Now situated on top was the last of the four volumes, a green-bound book with gold lettering, *Man And God*, by Gollancz. With a tilt of his head, he said to the camera, "Here we have a number of passages of great wisdom."

He opened the book about a quarter of the way, found his

page, and said, "On the very same page we have *The Talmud* telling us 'Him who destroys one human life, the Scripture regards as if he had destroyed the whole world.'

"Also, Berdyaev reminds us that 'The life and the destiny of the least of human beings has an absolute meaning in respect of eternity; his life and destiny are everlasting. For that reason he may not do away with a single human creature and escape punishment; we must consider the divine image and likeness in every one, from the most noble to the most despicable.'"

The deviant nodded his head. "What profound thoughts for us to dwell on. Now, after a brief message of interest to us all, we will be back with more."

He took the books, got up, and replaced them carefully in the top shelf of his bookcase. Then, from the top shelf, he took *The Imitation of Christ* by Thomas a Kempis, brought it back to his chair, and began to browse through it. As he read he muttered, "'...and many hear the world more gladly than Me, and more easily follow the likings of the flesh than the pleasure of God.'"

He read, "'The world promises things of small value, yet is served with great affection; but God promises high and eternal things, and the hearts of the people are slow and dull.'" He nodded. "Yes, their hearts are slow and dull, but their bodies are moving at high speed. That is why I have retreated to this monastery, to fast and meditate and pray."

He thumped his chest. "All for Jesus!" He slumped back in the chair, closed the book, and sighed. His breathing slowed, the vertical crease in his forehead almost flattened, his dark brown eyes became glazed, and he stared at the black velvet wall. "A monk? Yes, I am a monk in the Order of The Holy Chalice. I am a Brother.

"Fayne? I know nothing of any such name. As for me, I no longer have a formal name. Simply call me Brother, for that is what I am. Your name is Brother Favian? I do not recall any such name. The Home of The Holy Sepulchre? An orphanage? I know of no such place.

"My origin is not clear to me. I only know that I am content to be here in my hermitage. You say you are pleased that I received a vocation? You think I have done exceedingly well to have retreated from society and come closer to The Lord? I am pleased that you think well of me, but there is no need to praise me. I am a simple person following a simple course of action, or perhaps I should say a simple course of inaction.

"Yes, I will pray for you, Brother Favian, and I would appreciate it if you would pray for me as well. Oh...where?"

The glazed look began to leave his eyes, and he said, "The Brother is gone. It was good of him to come. He thought he knew me, but he was quite mistaken. Apparently I reminded him of someone he knew."

He got up from the scoop-back chair, went to the bookcase, replaced *The Imitation of Christ*, and walked slowly over to his washbowl. "It was good of him to come." At the washbowl he squirted the measured portions of liquid soap onto his hands, then rubbed the solution onto his palms and between his fingers. When he was finished washing, he muttered, "God is our loving Father."

Then he went to the dumbwaiter, removed a frozen food tray that was waiting there for him, heated it in the microwave oven, then stretched the tray's chain as far as it would go, to the utility table. There he sat on the stool and slowly ate half of the mashed potatoes, half of the sliced beets, half of the fishcake...and he drank exactly half of the decaffeinated coffee.

When he was done, leaving half of the meal behind him, he said, "It is good to avoid gluttony. It is wise to eat only enough to continue the functions of the body. Too much food is a burden for both the body and the mind." He bowed his head. "Thank you, Lord, for the gift of food that you have given to us, and thank you for the beverage you provided to accompany it. Thy will be done."

He went to the shower near the drain in the corner by his living area, removed his smock and slippers, lathered himself from head to foot with liquid soap from the nearby dispenser, and pressed the button to activate the shower. Then, for the precisely timed two-minute period which was always the duration of the shower, he scrubbed himself while chanting, "Shower us, O Lord, with your blessings. Shower us, O Lord, with your love. Shower us, O Lord, with your truth."

When the shower stopped, he waited a short while, chanting the same words in a singsong way. Then he pressed the soap dispenser button, lathered himself as before, showered himself, and continued the same washing process with every motion identical to the previous time.

He repeated this showering activity about ten times before he finally pressed the hot-air blow-drier button and dried himself, all the while chanting, "Shower us, O Lord, with your truth."

After putting on his smock and slippers, he went to the bookcase, took his leather-bound prayer book with the gold cross and the three candle symbols on the cover, went to the scoop-back chair and leafed through the pages until he found the section he was after.

Then he said aloud: "'My God, I offer Thee all the holy Masses which will be said this day throughout the whole world for poor sinners who are now in their death pangs and who will die this day. May the Precious Blood of our Savior Jesus Christ obtain for them mercy. Amen.'"

He nodded his head, turned back a page, and read, "'God, the singular protector of human weakness, hear, we beseech Thee, the prayers we humbly offer for those who'...oh?"

The door to his triangular-shaped unit clicked and buzzed and hummed and slid open. Sumner, his attendant, stepped inside. "Crap," he said as he looked around. "He's having another one of his clean fits." He sniffed the air with his parrot nose. "There's hardly anything here to clean up."

Doctor Fayne went back to the prayer book and began reading out loud again. "'...the prayers we humbly offer for those who are in peril, that Thou mayest save them from sin, and bring them into safety. Through Christ our Lord. Amen!'" He thumped his chest with his right fist. "Through Christ." He thumped his chest. "Our Lord." And again. "Amen!"

Sumner was hovering over him now, pointing toward the door. "I don't have time for that praying bunk, Fayne. The Kuh...Kuh...Keeper wants to see you, fella."

The deviant looked up at his short, broad-shouldered, sallow-complexioned attendant and said, "So it is you, Brother Summoner. You have come to pray with me in my hermitage. Kneel with me, Brother, and we will pray to The Lord together..."

"Listen, nut case, I told you I've got no time for that praying bunk, so get up and let's get going to The Clean Room." He pointed his index finger emphatically in front of the deviant's eyes. "Or else I'll have to stir up some juice to get you moving."

"Is it time for vespers? Or compline? Are we to gather in the cloister?"

"I'll vesper and compline your whole body, Fayne, if you don't get up and get going like I told you."

The deviant had a confused look as he rose slowly from the chair, whispering, "Brother Summoner must be under the weather. He seems dispirited. Out of sorts. Ill at ease." He looked into Sumner's vacant blue eyes and said, "I will go with you now to see Father Abbot. Thank you for coming to my hermitage to summon me, Brother. It was kind of you."

"Come on, Fayne. Get a move on." Sumner motioned for him to go through the doorway and out into the corridor. "And don't try that running away crap or your body will end up in The Trap."

Doctor Fayne, stepping into the corridor, said, "There is nothing for me to run away from. I am quite content here in my hermitage. As for traps and other pitfalls we may encounter on the road through life, I feel they are mainly creations of our own minds and that faith in Our Lord will always bring us to our eternal destination."

"You know, Fayne, I have never heard anyone talk as crazy as you. You're the most screwed-up nut case I've ever seen. Look, the Kuh...Kuh...Keeper doesn't like to be kept waiting. So get moving."

The deviant whispered, "It is interesting how he describes Father Abbot as The Keeper, and there may be merit to the designation, but I prefer the more traditional Father Abbot."

There was a slight, almost inaudible rumbling sound as a mild vibration went through the concrete under their feet. Sumner said, "It's probably the idiot FRN sympathizers again, making trouble in New Grafton. Well, they'll get theirs. They'll find their bodies in a Patho Shelter, where I'll get them and clean them and ship them off to war, and maybe I'll get a few to keep me company in the morgue here." He sniffed. "The morgue is so brand new and empty now. Not a stiff lying there."

"I am quite content to be here in my hermitage," said Doctor Fayne as he shuffled along. "Yes, Brother Summoner, I have no wants and no needs except to say my prayers and meditate and read my inspirational literature."

"How many times do I have to tell you, Fayne? My name isn't Suh-muh-ner, it's Sumner, and I am no Brother. What a screwed-up nut case. One time you call me Slumner and another time you call me Brother Suh-muh-ner. When are you going to get it straight, Fayne?"

The deviant dodged the question and said, "It will be good to join the others for the evening service. Although I prefer seclusion, it is good to see one's fellow man at vespers from time to time. It is an aid to the perspective, and it recalls the reality that we are all members of the Mystical Body of Christ, to which all Christians belong."

"Mystical bunk, Fayne. I never heard such crap. Anyhow, like I said, the FRN's stirring up trouble in the provinces. They'll never smarten up, the idiots. All they do is shaft themselves. You'd think they'd catch on, wouldn't you?"

The Doctor said nothing, and seemed to be whispering to himself as they walked along the corridor toward The Clean Room. Then Sumner said, "You don't give a crap about anything, do you, Fayne?"

The deviant remained silent as he walked along, with his lips moving ever so slightly, as if he might be praying to himself. "Ah, what's the use of talking to you, Fayne!" Sumner shook his head. "I never get an answer that makes any sense anyway. Get moving, nut case. We have to get you washed up so you can see The Kuh... Kuh...Keeper. "

Nothing else was said by either of them until they reached The Clean Room, where Sumner went through the customary routine of ordering him through the cleaning process, overseeing the shooting of a dose of tranquilizer into his arm, getting him washed and dried and into a clean smock and slippers, and motivating him to move in the direction of The Keeper's chamber.

"It is good to be scrubbed and showered and as clean in body as in spirit," said the deviant as they left The Clean Room and headed along the spotless corridor leading from there to The Keeper's chamber. "Cleanliness in the outer self is a fine accompaniment to cleanliness in the inner self."

The deviant did not say one more word to Sumner as they continued to The Keeper's chamber. But when they reached the point where the corridor leading to The Keeper went off at a sharp angle to the right, and the corridor going straight ahead disappeared into total darkness, Doctor Fayne stopped.

"Get going, Fayne," ordered Sumner. But the deviant

seemed confused, and began to go straight ahead into the dark corridor. Sumner growled, "The other way, nut case. That isn't the way to see The Kuh...Kuh...Keeper. That's the way to The Trap, you idiot." He pointed his finger at the deviant. "Get going down The Keeper's corridor to the gold door, nut case."

Slowly, the deviant shuffled toward the golden door, and The Keeper's amplified voice boomed out, "You may go now, Sumner. Come right ahead, Doctor Fayne. Come toward my golden door."

"Yes, Father Abbot."

The golden door clicked and buzzed and hummed, and slid open. When The Keeper ordered him to come in, he stepped through the opening and received the automated shots of memory stimulator and tranquilizer, threw himself on his knees on the metallic floor, and made the Sign of The Cross, saying loudly, "Bless me, Father, for I have sinned. It is quite some time since my last confession."

"This is no confessional, Doctor Fayne. This is the Psychological Deviant Shelter in Bentham, and you are experiencing Total Scrutiny methodology in conjunction with Time Void Therapy. Please dispense with the religious references. In The New Social System all that drivel has been abolished."

Doctor Fayne whispered, "Father Abbott seems confused. Perhaps he has been under too much pressure. I will try to be kind to him, and very humble, and I will pray for him."

The Keeper ordered Doctor Fayne to remove his slippers and place them at the edge of the oval gold velvet rug, which the deviant did without hesitation. As he placed his slippers near the oval rug, he said softly, " 'Silver hath beginnings of its veins, and gold a place wherein it is melted. Iron is taken out of the earth, and stone melted with heat is turned into brass. He hath set a time for darkness, and the end of all things he considereth, the stone also that is in the dark, and the shadow of death.' Thy will be done, O Lord, Our Loving Father. Thy will be..."

"Stop your muttering, Doctor. Go to the three steps and kneel on the second step." The deviant began to cross the rug, and when he felt the sensual stimulation of the fabric, he made the Sign of The Cross several times and then he said over and over, "Lead us not into temptation."

He was almost to the steps when he suddenly stopped and cocked his head to one side, as if listening to someone talk. He said, "Anna? I do not recall the name. You love me? Why, that is very nice of you to say that. We must all love one another. Husband? No. I could never be a husband. You see, I am a Brother in The Order of The Holy Chalice.

"I am a simple contemplative monk. I am a recluse, my dear. Happiness? The only happiness for me, my dear, is closeness to The Lord. But I do appreciate your kind words. I...oh, she has gone. It is strange how my visitors come and go so abruptly. But it is good of them to think of me. It is..."

"Kneel on the second step without further delay," ordered The Keeper. Doctor Fayne complied. His eyes were in an appropriately glazed state, and he was in a loose, slumped posture as he stared at the blurry golden circle in the center of the translucent golden wall.

When Doctor Fayne gave visual proof that he would now be compliant enough to continue, The Keeper said, "During your last session with me, you were telling me about the four variations of Anna...the conservative social worker, the pleasure addict, the woman in the white dress who thought she was your abandoned bride, and the depressed widow. You were saying that Anna the widow was in such a state of torment that her facial structure was changing. What kind of a look did she have, Doctor?"

The deviant nodded, the crease in his forehead began to flatten out slightly, and his face looked less bewildered now. "She had a demonic look, filled with hatred. She looked exactly like a cornered she-wolf. It was horrible. Her hollow-looking eyes filled with a strange new light, like the reflections in a wolf's eyes during the full moon.

"She began looking at me without blinking, her cheekbones became more prominent, her teeth even developed a canine look. On the one hand she seemed more and more overwhelmed by her fears, and on the other I detected a dangerous hatred in those beast-like eyes.

"I thought about putting her in an institution, but I couldn't accept the idea at first, even though Anna terrified me more and more every time I saw her. The situation had me in a complete muddle. What could I do with her? Or should I say *them*?

"When she was the social worker she was hardly a problem at all. But Anna the pleasure addict, even though she always avoided me by using the outside stairway, was becoming more raucous and degraded with each passing day. Anna-of-the-white-bridal-dress was demented. And the widow with her inner darkness was becoming a very dangerous person.

"There was nobody I could turn to with my problem. The people in the local neighborhood couldn't have cared less about her being mad. In fact, they may have enjoyed the idea of the Doctor having a mad wife.

"Finally, she became so violent that I had no other choice but to have her consigned to a Pathological Deviant Shelter. I had to do that. An evil essence had imbedded itself in her mind. She had become a hazard to her existence and mine.

"She was threatening me with death constantly, spewing her hatred at me, attacking me physically and mentally, and torturing me with constant accusations about events that had never happened. She was wearing me out. Exhausting me.

"Having her put away was the most difficult thing I have ever experienced. And from that day forward I have been haunted by her screams and her accusations and that demented demonic face with its look of...its look of..." He shook his head and the crease in his forehead deepened. "Her once beautiful face took on...her face...her face..."

"Doctor Fayne," said The Keeper with a warmth in his voice that was not customary. "I want to thank you for sharing your truth with me. You have earned the privilege of ascending to the third step. Please rise."

The deviant got up slowly and with a bewildered look on his face, he stood near the bottom of the steps. The automated armrest mechanism went into action and moved up along its track to the top step. "Kneel on the top step now," ordered The Keeper. Doctor Fayne complied.

"In a moment we will complete The Unveiling, Doctor." The deviant nodded his head. "But first I must obtain a computer analysis of our progress to see if there are any matters that need further clarification."

Then came a series of clicking and whirring sounds as the computer did its work. Finally, The Keeper announced, "Apparently we have been as complete as is practicable during our dialogues. The computer alerts us to a number of inconsistencies within the framework of your personality, but the inconsistencies are part and parcel of your deviant condition. As far as our dialogue has been concerned we have been completely consistent.

"Of some concern to us, Doctor, is the critical tone of your statements on the obvious economic facts of our evolutionary process. However, we do understand how your religious orientation has colored your views. Naturally, for you to function in a wholesome way in our society your views must be modified. We have a new therapeutic process which we believe will accomplish that, and I am very sure that the new process will be beneficial for you.

"Now, Doctor Fayne, we enter the ultimate phase of The Unveiling. We have succeeded in moving you to the third step because the intent of The Unveiling has been accomplished. We have found out all we wished to learn. We are confident that you are not Lance Crowne, the public enemy. Yes, that is what they have been calling you, Doctor. If we had not intervened, they would have killed you that day when we found you besieged on all sides.

"Instead, it was your good fortune to be consigned to the new Psychological Deviant Shelter in Bentham for observation and therapy. Now, Doctor, it appears there is hope for your complete rehabilitation. In due course you should once again be a useful contributor to the economy.

"According to our diagnostic computer, Doctor, you are suffering from a rare mental malady called enantiodromia. Apparently, this syndrome was brought about by the shock of your distressing experiences with Anna. When your wife's psyche broke into unrelated segments, the effect of your exposure to such a personality fragmentation was disastrous.

"As a kind of defense, you fell into enantiodromia, a morbid fascination with opposites, to such a degree that your own personality split off into fragments. Your rehabilitation has been challenging, but we now have a substantial amount of hope. So let us proceed. Look at the wall ahead of you. Examine it closely."

The deviant's dark brown eyes focused on the translucent golden screen-like wall as it began to radiate a much brighter glow than usual. Then an image began to appear directly over the area where the blurry golden circle was located.

"Examine the image in the center of the screen, Doctor. At first it may seem confusing and perhaps even chaotic, but The Screen of Truth never lies. Look closely at the image, Doctor Fayne, and tell me what you see."

As the deviant squinted, the vertical crease in his forehead deepened. Then his face contorted with disdain and he said, "It's a...I think it's...it's a very repulsive creature." He shook his head and closed his eyes.

"Open your eyes, Doctor. Very rarely does anyone have

the opportunity to view The Screen of Truth as you are now doing. Please continue to observe that image on the screen even though it may repel you."

Opening his eyes, he examined the image on the screen. Again he shook his head and closed his eyes. Then he said, "It's one of the most nauseating creatures I've ever seen."

The Keeper said, "Your reaction is to be expected. But now I want you to open your eyes and accept what you see instead of questioning it or rejecting it. Describe exactly what you see."

The deviant opened his eyes and focused his attention on the glowing portion of the translucent screen-like wall, and he said, "It looks like a huge head...with all kinds of features that don't belong together. It's hard to tell if it's the head of a person or an animal or some other kind of creature.

"The basic shape of the head is like a...like a lion, I think. And the eyes are the eyes of a fox. The ears look like a...let's see, are they like a rabbit's ears or are they...yes, that's it, they're the ears of a mule. And the hair is like...yes, it's like a lamb's hair. The part that looks like a face seems to be some kind of lizard's face...or is it a...yes, I think it's the face of a chameleon."

"Doctor Fayne," said The Keeper," you are absolutely right about the constituent parts of the image. Now tell me, do you recognize anything meaningful about the image?"

"No."

"Keep looking closely at the image, Doctor. You will soon see what you are supposed to see. You must try to understand that nothing in this life is as it seems. For example, a smooth pond on a windless day looks solid, but if you step on that water you will rapidly sink in the liquid. It is similar with human beings, Doctor.

"We suffer from perceptions that combine illusion and reality. For each normal person there are always two images: one an illusion and the other real. In ordinary life the faces we see are only illusions and the reality always escapes us. You, Doctor, are now looking at The Screen of Truth, which never lies and always reflects reality instead of illusion. Look closely at the image. Tell me whose reality you see."

The deviant squinted at first, then opened his eyes wide and stared at the blurry golden circle. Then he began to shudder as he muttered, "No, it...it can't be..."

"Accept what you see, Doctor, and tell me who it is."

"It's...it's me!"

"Yes, Doctor, it is your own image that you see. It is not the illusion that you present to other people. That strange combination of attributes that you see before you on The Screen of Truth reflects the essential you. Do you still find it repulsive?"

"Very much so."

"Doctor, as we work to assist you toward your full potential, your image will grow on you. Our basic purpose here is to help you become very healthy. As you know, we are quite concerned about you. But since you have reached the third step we believe your rehabilitation will move forward rapidly.

"It should please you to know that the commission overseeing your case has taken a special interest in you. Soon you will be the first person to experience our new Cranial Reorganization Therapy, or CRT.

"After your deviant tendencies are resolved, our specialists will prepare you for useful employment. Because of your experience as publisher of your own *Journal* and your contacts with mass media, the commissioners have decided that you will be employed as Public Information Director for The Deviant Shelter League."

Instead of reacting with pleasure to this great honor, a look of shock and horror came over the deviant's face. Then his voice faltered and Doctor Fayne said tremulously, " 'Over all the glory shall be a protection. And there shall be a tabernacle for a shade in the daytime from the heat, and for a security and covert from the whirlwind, and from rain...'"

"What are you saying, Doctor?" asked The Keeper. "Are you drifting off? Please stay with our dialogue. It will benefit you greatly, I assure you."

The deviant said, "'And there shall be a tabernacle for a shade in the daytime from the heat, and for a security and...'"

"Your comments have no relevance to our discussion," said The Keeper with some irritation. "You must try to relate to what I am saying to you. Now I will give you a moment to see if you can compose yourself."

After a very brief pause, Doctor Fayne, with heavy-lidded eyes gazing at the blurry golden circle in the center of the screen-like wall, said in a singsong voice, "'We have a building from God, a house not made by human hands, eternal in the heavens. And indeed, in this present state we groan, yearning to be clothed over with that dwelling of ours which is from heaven, if indeed we shall be found clothed, and not naked. For we who are...'"

The Keeper interrupted him. "Cease this religious babbling, Doctor! Why are you lapsing into Biblical quotations? I have no time for such drivel. Now please attempt to focus your attention on our dialogue. Are you ready to continue?"

"Yes, Father Abbot, I will continue with my prayers. 'Behold, he comes with the clouds, and every eye shall see him, and they also who pierced him. And all the tribes of the earth shall wail over him. Even so. Amen. I am the Alpha and the Omega, the beginning and the end, says the Lord God, who is and who was and who is coming, the Almighty.'"

"Apparently our session is over, Doctor," said The Keeper. "I cannot tolerate any more of this inane babbling. If you want to babble on, do so in your seclusion where you will not offend my sensitive ears. Please go now, and put on

your slippers, and return with Sumner to your triangle."
Doctor Fayne nodded his head and said calmly, "Yes,
Father Abbot." Then he crossed the rug, became sensually
stimulated, made the Sign of The Cross several times, and
muttered, "Lead us not into temptation."
He went to his slippers, put them on, then threw himself
on his knees on the hard gold metallic floor, saying, "Behold,
our loving Savior comes with the clouds. Thank you, Lord,
for all the blessings you have bestowed on me."
"Go now, Doctor!" There was strong irritation in The
Keeper's voice. "Go to your triangle...and rest. I order you to
rise. You must rejoin Sumner, who will lead you back to
your triangle."
"Yes, Father Abbot. I will rejoin Brother Summoner and
return to my hermitage."
He put on his slippers and shuffled toward the sliding
golden door, then waited. After a click and a buzz and a
hum, the door slid open and The Keeper said, "Go to your
triangle and rest. Go now!"
"Yes, Father Abbot." The deviant nodded his head slowly.
"I thank you, Father Abbot. May God bless you, and please
pray for me so that I will rest in peace."
He stepped out into the corridor and the golden door slid
closed behind him. He shuffled along the short corridor to its
junction with the main corridor where Sumner was waiting
for him. When he reached Sumner, he said, "How nice of
you to walk and pray with me, Brother Summoner. You are
far kinder than I deserve."
Sumner spoke abruptly to the deviant. "Get going, nut
case, and never mind that crazy talk." The attendant pointed
to the dark extension of the main corridor. "Keep talking like
that and your body is going to be right down there in the new
CRT unit before you know it.
"Do you know what CRT is, Fayne? It's called Cranial
Reorganization Therapy. They say it's really going to be

something special when they do it. It's going to straighten out people's heads and re-educate them. If they can't straighten out their heads it's going to be into The Trap with them, and then to the morgue, and then nothing but ashes."

Doctor Fayne looked with wide eyes toward the enveloping blackness of that corridor where he had found himself drawn earlier, on the way to The Keeper's chamber, only to be redirected toward his destination by Sumner.

Again he was drawn toward that mysterious darkness and instead of following Sumner along the main corridor, as directed, he turned and began to shuffle toward the endless blackness.

"All right, nut case, you're asking for it," muttered Sumner as he leaped past the deviant and stood between him and the darkness. "Get your stupid body back into the main corridor." He pointed his hand at the deviant's legs, waved the hand to administer the shock, and Doctor Fayne grunted, "Hrgh!" and jumped toward the main corridor.

Sumner remained behind him as they walked toward the deviant's triangle, and every few paces he pointed his hand at the deviant's buttocks to motivate him. Each time Doctor Fayne grunted and shuddered, Sumner said, "That'll show you what happens to guys that don't go along with what they're told. A little juice might help you remember which way you're going. Why did you want to go down that black corridor anyway, huh?"

"I was going to meditate there, Brother Summoner."

"That's just bunk, you lying nut case."

Finally they reached the deviant's triangle and they both stopped in front of the sliding door. But Sumner did not insert the key into the lock-switch. Instead he thrust his face up toward Doctor Fayne's and said "All right, Fayne, now this is it."

He raised his hand and pointed it toward the deviant's genitals. "You're going to get the full treatment, fella, right in the balls if you don't tell me why you wanted to go down that black corridor." He stood back slightly and pointed at Doctor Fayne's genitals. "Are you going to answer me or not?"

Doctor Fayne said softly, "Answer you, Brother Summoner? What is it that I must answer you about? I have been meditating, you see, and have heard no question."

"You better not be putting me on, Fayne, so here's the question for the last time, nut case." He repeated the question.

The deviant said calmly, "Why, Brother Summoner, I was simply going into the dark chapel to say a prayer and light a candle."

"You expect me to fall for that bunk?" replied Sumner.

"I do not understand the words you are using to communicate with me, Brother Summoner. Are you in danger of falling? There do not appear to be any obstacles near your feet."

"Ah crap, it's no use talking to you, Fayne. I've never seen anyone so screwed up as you. If you don't end up getting that new CRT therapy or thrown in The Trap, they'll probably ship you off to a patho shelter one of these days." He inserted his key into the lock and activated the sliding door. "Get your body in there, Fayne."

The deviant entered his triangle and as the door slid closed behind him he turned to Sumner, who remained in the corridor, and he said, "Thank you for accompanying me on my prayer walk, Brother Summoner. It was kind of you to spend your time with me."

"Think nothing of it, nut case," said Sumner as the door closed. "It's my job."

Doctor Fayne was all alone again, sealed into his triangle. As he walked slowly toward his book case he appeared more haggard than ever, with his face very pale and his mouth hanging open slightly from exhaustion. "I do not understand much of what Brother Summoner says to me," he muttered.

"I have difficulty absorbing his speech pattern. Apparently I do not have the gift of speaking in tongues or understanding various tongues."

Taking his Bible, he returned with it to the scoop-back gray plastic chair and methodically began to turn the pages to the section he was after. "Here we are, Luke Twenty-One. A section of considerable interest to all of us."

He sighed, nodded, and fixed his eyes on the nearest television camera. "It is written that 'the days will come in which there will not be left one stone upon another that will not be thrown down.' These are not pleasant words to contemplate, yet the Lord has spoken them for our benefit because He wishes to prepare us for the life to come by reminding us that the life we now live may end abruptly and things we look upon as permanent are not permanent at all.

"'Nation will rise against nation, and kingdom against kingdom; and there will be great earthquakes in various places, and pestilences and famines, and there will be terrors and great signs from heaven,' He is telling us that the end will come, and before the end we will be faced with much unpleasantness. He even tells us that we will be arrested and persecuted for his name's sake, but all for a purpose! 'It shall lead to your bearing witness.'"

Fixing his gaze on the camera lens, he asked, "Have you borne witness lately? Have you turned to your neighbor and said, 'I believe in The Lord Jesus?' Have you spoken to God in your prayers and said, 'Thy will be done'? You see, if you believe in the Lord Jesus you have nothing to fear from the tumbling stones and the warring nations and the upheavals of the earth and all the other signs from heaven. If you bear witness, and believe in him with all your heart, you will be prepared."

His eyes widened and he took a deep breath. Then he looked down at the Bible again, and read, " 'Not a hair of your head shall perish. By your patience you will win your souls.'"

As his eyes fixed on the lens of the video camera, it seemed as if he were gazing off into infinity. "Patience, my friends. You must have patience."

He rose from the chair, with the Bible in his hands, and then he dropped to his knees. With his eyes toward the camera he said softly, "Join me in saying 'I believe in you, Jesus. Forgive this thy humble servant for his sins which are so numerous.'" He breathed deeply and slowly as he said, "I love you, Lord Jesus, and I love our Father in Heaven."

Kneeling there, he put the Bible in his left hand, and he muttered "Thy" while thumping his chest with his right fist. He muttered "will" and thumped his chest again. He said "be," thumping his chest a third time. Then, with trembling lips, and two tears flowing down his cheeks, he said "done."

"Yes," he said, "I am nearly done. Soon my brain will be reorganized and they will re-educate me. They will help me to fit the current definition of normal and guide me into being more useful to the economy."

Sighing, he bowed almost to the floor as he kneeled there, never taking his eyes from the camera. Finally he nodded shakily, and with quivering lips he said, "Now for a brief pause for a message of interest to us all. We will be back with more shortly. Please stay with us."

He was holding The Bible against his chest as he prayed, almost inaudibly. "The Lord be with us as we move toward union with His loving heart. Protect us and guide us, O Lord, as we attempt to humbly do your will in all things. Thank you for this hermitage. Thank you for your love. Thank you for everything."

Then a change in the deviant's disposition occurred. His shaky, apprehensive mood faded and was replaced by a calm demeanor. A serene smile appeared on Doctor Fayne's face as he said confidently, "I am yours to use exactly as you wish, Lord. Thy will be done...always. And when my work here on Earth is done, may I rest…rest in peace."

Case Report Disposition

Having engaged in considerable observation, and having achieved our basic objectives, a change in therapy is now recommended for the delusional deviant. First, Time Void Therapy is to be terminated. Then CRT is to be applied. Our new Cranial Reorganization Therapy should rapidly bring Doctor Fayne to optimum utility and emotional balance as he prepares for his new assignment as the Public Information Director for The Deviant Shelter League. His talents as a professor and a writer will be very helpful in his new role. It is confidently expected that with appropriate guidance the deviant will soon be transformed into a very useful member of society and a distinct asset to the economy of the United Econocratic Provinces.

…the end…

About the Author

The 25th Anniversary issue of *Cape Cod Life Magazine* selected Tom O'Connell as "one of the top 100 influential people" on Cape Cod. Also, he is listed in *Who's Who in the East.*

Tom is a Cape Cod Writer, Lecturer and Educator. Take a look at his sanctuary777.com website where you will find many essays as well as excerpts from his books.

A Few Facts

Bachelor of Arts *cum laude*. History & Government. Boston College, College of Arts & Sciences.

Master of Arts. History. (U.S. and European). Boston University, The Graduate School of Arts & Sciences.

Served as School Committee Chairman, Town Meeting Member, Political Campaign Organizer, Lobbyist.

Formerly the CEO of four different organizations in the automotive industry, long term health care, public housing, and accident prevention.

Independent Freelance Writer & Editor since 1978.

Publisher, *Lifestyle Journal* at www.sanctuary777.com.

His website provides excerpts from his books and some 200 lifestyle essays emphasizing addiction and recovery.

Past President, American Medical Writers Association, New England Chapter. Member (1980-   ).

English Professor, Adjunct Faculty, Cape Cod Community College (1988-2007).

Writing Tutor/Mentor, Cape Cod Community College (1991-2010).

Member, Cape Cod Writers' Center (1981-   ). Served as Board member and Program Planner.

National Correspondent, *U.S. Journal of Drug & Alcohol Dependence* (1983-1991).

Columnist, *Cape Cod Times* (1986-1999).

Columnist, *Cape Cod Journal* (1999-2000).

Columnist, *The Cape Codder* (2000-2005).

Political Commentator, campaign2america.com (2007-2008).

Member, Secular Franciscan Order (S.F.O.) (1980-   ).

email: info@sanctuary777.com
Website: www.sanctuary777.com
PO Box 25, Dennisport, MAssachusetts 02639, USA

Sanctuary Unlimited Books by Tom O'Connell
Inspiration/Spirituality/Personal Growth/Entertainment
Review excerpts at sanctuary777.com
Buy at amazon.com or sanctuary777.com
email: info@sanctuary777.com

Deviant Shelter:
Year Three of The New Social System (NSS)
A Novel by Tom O'Connell

It is Year Three of The New Social System (NSS) and all mental health institutions, prisons and correctional facilities in the United Econocratic Provinces have been replaced with deviant shelters for those who do not fit the government's current definition of the word "normal."

Doctor Wylie Fayne, a philosophy professor, is the first resident of a new psychological deviant shelter with highly advanced technology. He is housed in a triangular-shaped unit in the Total Scrutiny Wing of the granite shelter constructed as a pyramid.

The professor has the distinction of being the first to experience the new Time Void Therapy. Neuropsychological implants (NPI) have been attached to his nervous system. The goal of his therapy is to move him toward an acceptable mental condition so he can be useful to the government.

Comments on the Author's Books~~"Tom O'Connell connects with readers soul to soul...inspires."--Jordan Rich, *WBZ News Radio 1030,* Boston. "O'Connell writes compellingly."--Melanie Lauwers, *Cape Cod Times.* ($17)

To order books, refer your bookseller to
Ingram Book Company or go to amazon.com
or place your order through sanctuary777.com

Power, Politics & Propaganda:
Observations of a Curious Contrarian
This collection of thought-provoking essays is a reminder about the importance of individual liberty in a world moving toward more systems of government putting the group first.

O'Connell explores how power, politics and propaganda lead to supremacy of the collective over the free individual.

The danger, he contends, is that despite allegedly good intentions the elite collectivists and secularists are apt to consider those who believe in God as candidates for the Flat Earth Society.

O'Connell's key philosophy: "Individual liberty is our birthright... Respect for life is the key to both individual liberty and group harmony."

He says a Divine Plan is at work in the destinies of individuals and nations. Unimpressed with mob dynamics, he stresses individual liberty.

Comments on the Author's Books~~"Tom O'Connell connects with readers soul to soul...inspires."--Jordan Rich, *WBZ News Radio 1030,* Boston. "O'Connell writes compellingly."--Melanie Lauwers, *Cape Cod Times.* "Very vivid...fascinating."--Bob Silverberg, *Books & The World TV.* "Compelling and inspiring."--Ed Maroney, *The Barnstable Patriot* ($17)

Bugging Out: An Army Memoir (1954)

With wit and irony, the author uses candid dialogue and vivid descriptions to tell how he dealt with the military assaults on his independent personality.

As a "voluntary" draftee with a pregnant wife, he is demoralized by cruel superiors and caught between duty and self-preservation. Reluctantly, he turns to "bugging out" as he tries to cope with the Army's challenges to his sanity. Scenes reflect outrage, despair, and hilarity.

"Tom's memoirs are written like novels."--Jordan Rich, *WBZ News Radio* 1030, Boston. "Very vivid...a fascinating read."--*Books & The World TV.* "A real picture of what it was like...no holds barred." -- *Provincetown Banner.* "A let-it-all-hang-out memoir ...interesting characters."--*Barnstable Patriot.* ($17)

The O'Connell Boy: Educating "The Wolf Child" ~ *An Irish-American Memoir (1932-1950)*

Lively impressions of a "wolf child" life in homes with solitary Irish immigrant women. Nine years at Mrs. White's "lace curtain Irish" Catholic Charities group home. Her perfectionist "reign of terror." Then a "free" teen's "battle of wits" with Irish granny on "the other side of the tracks."

"Tom O'Connell connects with readers soul to soul...inspires."--Jordan Rich, *WBZ News Radio* 1030, Boston. "a page-turner...heart wrenching... mind boggling...stunning."--*Cape Cod Magazine.* "a fascinating memoir...a charming and honest writing voice."--*The Cape Codder.* "O'Connell writes compellingly..."--*Cape Cod Times.* "compelling and inspiring."--*The Barnstable Patriot.* ($17)

Improving Intimacy: 10 Powerful Strategies
~A Spiritual Approach

A look at spiritually based intimacy, addictive relating, control, listening, communication, conflict. 10 strategies for healthy, loving relationships. **"Positive...powerful...very readable style."**--*Cape Cod Times.* **"It's the finest example of anyone writing on this subject."--Don LaTulippe, WPLM, Plymouth. ($10)**

The Odd Duck: A Story for Odd People of All Ages

A cheerful, inspiring fable for "adult children." A lost duck raised in a chicken coop feels odd. After an identity crisis, a quest for self-worth brings healthy, lasting love.

 "A cheerful, punning little allegory mostly for grownups."--*Bostonia Magazine.* **"a parable for spiritual reawakening."--***Seniors Cape Cod Forum.* **($10)**

Danny The Prophet: A Fantastic Adventure

A man reluctant to be God's last prophet has more worldly plans. A fantastic journey: a politician, a sage, an angel, many perilous adventures, divine revelations.

 Readers' say: "Astounding!" "Wow!" "Funny!" "A wonderful book!" "A pleasure to read!" ($17)

The Monadnock Revelations: A Spiritual Memoir

The true story of Tom's mystical journey. A special hour with God in the Monadnock Mountains. A report on Cosmic Consciousness. Divine revelations.

 Readers' comments: "Encourages, energizes and inspires..." "It warmed my heart and inspired my soul." "A treasury of inspiration." "I loved it!" "Extremely visionary, well written, inspiring...a great book." ($17)

Addicted?: A Guide to Understanding Addiction
A practical guide toward greater understanding of the addictions. Alcohol, drugs, gambling, relationships, etc.
   "A wealth of information ...highly readable" --Blaise Gambino, Ph.D., Director of Research & Education, Gambling Program, Harvard Medical School. ($20)

Up In Smoke: The Nicotine Challenge in Recovery
Nearly 20,000 of these motivational booklets originally published by Hazelden were used in smoking cessation programs to help recovering alcoholics to also quit smoking! Hazelden has returned all rights to the author. **($7)**

Note:

When ordering directly from sanctuary777.com, pay by check and add $5 to each price for shipping and handling.

To use credit card, go to amazon.com.

**To order books, refer your bookseller to
Ingram Book Company or go to amazon.com
or place your order through sanctuary777.com**

Thank you!

Your comments on this book will be much appreciated!

---

email: info@sanctuary777.com, Website: sanctuary777.com
PO Box 25, Dennisport, MAssachusetts 02639, USA

NOTES

LaVergne, TN USA
07 June 2010
185314LV00001B/49/P

ISBN 9 780982 776605

Breinigsville, PA USA
04 November 2010
248682BV00001B/4/P